Loose Ends

GUY CULLEN

authorHOUSE®

AuthorHouse™ UK Ltd.
500 Avebury Boulevard
Central Milton Keynes, MK9 2BE
www.authorhouse.co.uk
Phone: 08001974150

First published by AuthorHouse 9/9/2008

ISBN: 978-1-4343-9038-7 (sc)

Printed in the United States of America
Bloomington, Indiana

This book is printed on acid-free paper.

For my son Ethan, to whom I owe my liberty and my life.

Thanks to...

Tony Loftus, Manni (Dave Mansfield), Neil Thomas, Bigsy (Mike Biglands), Mike Quinn, Rachel Hall, Aly Hodgson, Geoff Hodgson, Barbara Skinner, Simon Ross, Gary Hinks, Kev Seed, Dean Sullivan and last but by no means least, Lorna and Andy Haynes.

Prologue

CONSCIOUSNESS RETURNS AND THE SIGHT that greets me is a gruesome one.

How did it come to this? How did I allow myself to get to this point? These are questions I just can't answer.

To make any sense of it all I need to go back to a time when things were ordinary, to a time when I was ordinary, but everything's changed so much now that it's hard to remember the way I was before all this started.

They say ignorance is bliss, out of sight out of mind, what the eye doesn't see, the heart doesn't grieve over, but I've done more than my fair share of grieving if the truth be known. I grieve every day, for the people I've lost and the life I've squandered. I grieve for the part of me that was naïve to this side of life which I now find myself consumed by.

I don't suppose I'm making much sense here and you'd be forgiven for thinking I'm a little unhinged. Truth is you may be right. Truth is I've seen and done things from which there is no return.

Was I ever ordinary or was this part of me lurking beneath the surface, waiting to emerge at the appropriate time? Would I have lived my life never knowing of my other side if I had not made the choices I did?

And how simple those choices were. No long contemplation, no great deliberation. I made my choices simply and quickly with no apparent regard for the consequences and no conception of the fallout that would inevitably ensue. But that's me all over, act first, ask questions later. Impulsive isn't in it.

The blood's starting to dry now. It's russet hue covering my hands and forearms. I can feel it hardening on my face as it oxidises and clots.

There's no way back from this. There's no way I can ever live a normal life again, not knowing what I know now. Not having done what I've done and seen what I've seen. But I can't complain. It was all of my own doing, all my own choice and now I must take the consequences.

CHAPTER 1

Nine Months Earlier...

I AM COLD. No, I am freezing. Absolutely, positively, unbelievably freezing. The numbness is spreading from my toes, through my feet and into my shins despite my best efforts to keep the blood flowing.

This has got to be the longest winter we've had for years. Longest and coldest, although, you'd never know it by the clothes some of these girls are wearing. It would seem that nobody bothered to tell them it's winter at all. Look at them, clacking along the pavement in their micro skirts and miniscule tops. Acres of skin open to the elements as they soldier on from one bar to another. Not into here though. The classy one's very rarely come into this dive and if they ever do, they don't stay for long. Not the most reputable establishment in the city this one. Full of plastic gangsters and little rats in hoodies. The dregs of this fair city seem to congregate here every weekend and lucky me gets to stand on the door and watch them bounce in with their put on limps and moody faces.

Fact is I fucking hate the place but it's money isn't it? It keeps the wolves from the door at the end of the day and that's all that matters. I'll stand here every weekend if I have to if it means putting food on the table and paying the bills, but that's all it is to me.

You can keep all the macho bollocks that goes with the job. I can't be arsed who thinks what of me to be perfectly honest and I have no time for those that are.

Some fellas, like the one stood next to me tonight, see this as something to be proud of, as a career. Fucking sad if you ask me. Putting yourself on offer night after night for a couple of quid does not go down as something to be proud of in my book. It's a means to an end is all it is. When you've got a young family, you do the best you can don't you? And if that means freezing my knackers off on this shithole then so be it.

This lad does really buzz off all this though. Look at him there, Big cheesy grin slapped all over his grid. Can hardly contain his elation even though it's minus three. I suppose he's only young, twenty-one at a push. I bet all his mates are dead proud of the fact that they knock around with a lad who works for Henry Haynes. That's our boss by the way, big H. Looks like The Thing, massive shoulders, no neck and a head like a cannonball. One tough cookie is H. Nasty piece of work. Not to be fucked about with under any circumstances and I try to keep things on a purely business level with the fella. I turn up on time, do my job, collect my money and that's me done. I've no desire to knock around the office like some of the lads seem to do, waiting for the proverbial scraps off the table, wanting to be seen to be socialising with the big fella. Can't be arsed with all that brown nosing caper myself. The only reason I go into that office is to get my wages then I'm out of there. Goodnight Vienna.

This cold weather's killing me tonight though. Think I might be getting too old for all of this carry on. Might have to find another source of income to swell the coffers. Doesn't seem to be bothering Kieran that much. That's his name by the way, my partner in crime for the evening, Kieran Jacobs. Reckons his uncle's Jerry Jacobs, but then everybody reckons they're related to Jerry Jacobs. In fact, if everybody that claimed to be related to the legendary grafter actually was, he'd have a bigger family than the Waltons.

Jerry Jacobs my arse. If he was JJ's nephew he wouldn't be working this dump that's for sure. He keeps trying to regale me with tales of bravado from other doors but I think he's getting the message that I'm not all that interested. Not being funny but I've heard it all before.

Kieran turns to say something to me but is interrupted by the sight of one of the DJs panting his way up the stairs with a look of horror on his dial.

"It's all going off down there lads, some cunt's been bottled!" he gasps as he struggles to draw breath.

Instinctively we pile down the stairs and onto the dance floor looking for the poor sod who's bleeding.

As we approach him I notice a gang of lads stood off to his left, all snarling with attitude written all over their screwed up, twisted faces. There's about ten of them. Hardly fair odds. And the lad's in a terrible mess, half of his nose looks like it's hanging off and there's blood absolutely everywhere.

One of the gang of grocks breaks away from the group to come and have a conspiratorial word with yours truly. He places his hand on my arm and leans into my ear to be heard above the thump, thump of R and B music.

"You wanna get him out of here la" He suggests, with his best menacing tone "Lad's gonna get fucked if he stays around much longer"

"Oh aye?" I reply turning to the injured punter.

"You alright?" I ask him, he's obviously pretty fucking far from alright but you have to ask don't you? The lad just stands there dazed and confused, swaying slightly.

As I look around and take in the situation it dawns on me that, much as it pains me to agree, the best course of action is to get the casualty out to save any further damage. These lads look like they haven't finished with the poor cunt yet and the last thing we want is anymore bother in here.

"Come on then lad" I tell the injured drinker as I guide him over towards the stairs "Kieran get his other arm"

Now the look of confusion on his face deepens as he struggles to work out why he's being ejected when he is the victim. I know this is unfair but it's damage limitation isn't it? I think I've just recognised a few of the grocks and if they are who I think they are then this lad'll thank me for getting him the fuck out of the way.

Kieran grabs his other arm and as we lead him towards the stairs, a lad sitting on his own casually puts his pint down and gives the already wounded punter a dig square on the jaw. Not the fastest punch I've ever seen but it has the desired effect. The lad's knees buckle and we struggle to keep him upright.

The mystery assailant nonchalantly sits back down and continues with his pint. Cheeky bastard!

We make haste now and get the profusely bleeding, bewildered man to the top of the stairs and out of the door.

I feel a bit sorry for him as we leave him to his own devices and charge back into the club.

As we reach the bottom of the stairs again I grab the pint off the attacker and tell him "You're out of here for a start"

"Why's that like?" he asks, his face contorted with the injustice of it all.

"You know why, come on" I tell him as we take an arm each.

"Get your fuckin' hands off me" he screams as he tries to lash out but we've got him too tightly and all he succeeds in doing is wriggling enough for us to get his arms behind his back.

"Fuckin' move" Kieran shouts into his ear as we march him up the stairs.

Somehow I'm aware of the bottle a split second before it hits the back of my head. Just enough time to brace slightly as the dark green glass cascades all around me. The pain that flares outwards and downwards is exquisite and it's all I can do to keep my feet.

Of course he was with the other lads, fucking obvious wasn't it? Bad mistake kidder, very bad.

We turn our captive around to use as a shield against the on-slaught as we stagger backwards up the stairs and as if by magic, Henry Haynes appears behind us like Mr Ben's shopkeeper. He brushes past us without a word and wades into the now retreating gang with massive roundhouse punches that cause untold damage when they land.

The gang of grocks aren't so hard now and they flee in all directions in a frantic search for the back door, but Henry doesn't let up. He just keeps on after them, wounding and maiming indiscriminately.

I shove the lad's head into the banister hard enough to render him unconscious and go to join my psychotic boss as he culls the vermin.

A fair few of them are spark out on the floor but there's still a number of them left searching for a way out of this hell that they've suddenly found themselves in. No way out of this though lads.

One tries to run past me in an attempt to make it to the stairs but I take his legs from under him and finish him off with a punch to the side of the head. The skin rips open in a gush of blood and his eyes roll back in his head. The possibility that I've killed the cunt flashes through my adrenalin fuelled mind but I dismiss it out of hand.

Women are screaming and punters are desperately trying to escape, to get out of the way of this mad man.

I spot one of the gang who is trying to blend into the crowd and pretend he's not with the rest of them, trying to tuck himself into a corner, out of the way. No chance dickhead. As I move towards him Kieran's already there, punching him time and time again. I can't hear above the din but I think the lad's crying out for mercy. No chance.

Then the lads off've next door turn up and it's all over.

Chapter 2

Pulling up outside ours my stomach starts to flip in anticipation of what Amy will say when she sees the stitches in the back of my head. She never wanted me to work on the doors in the first place and she has worried herself sick every night I've worked for the last six months. This will just be the cherry on the cake this will. She'll hit the fucking roof when she finds out about tonight's little adventure and she'll demand that I pack it in. I can't though. No-can-do I'm afraid. Without the door money we would go under, no two ways about it. This is a fact. She's not working at the mo' and isn't likely to be in the near future with two young kids to look after and one on the way and the money from my day job just isn't enough, so back to the doors I go.

She'll be fine once she's calmed down. She's going to have to be. We don't have a choice.

I look up at the bedroom window to see the bedside light's on like it always is. She'll pretend she's been asleep but I know she never does until I'm safely tucked up in bed. With a bit of luck she won't see my injury 'til tomorrow, which gives me a few hours of grace at least.

As I put my key in the door I can hear the dog winding himself up in the kitchen, his paws clicking on the laminate floor as he bounds about working himself up into a frenzy. Then I open the door and he's all over me. You'd think he hasn't seen another soul for months the way he carries on, wagging his tale until he almost loses his balance.

I make a fuss of him then let him out the back door into the garden while I get myself a bowl of Weetabix. As I'm slurping them down, I catch sight of my reflection in the window. The large white pad is protruding from my bonce in quite a visible manner. I hope she's got her back to me when I go in the bedroom, that way I can just slide under the sheets and cuddle up to her. She won't turn round then. She'll just nod off when she knows I'm safe. I know she only worries because she cares and if there was any other way I could make this kind of money doing these hours at these times I would jump at it. Unfortunately there isn't.

I let the dog back in, creep up the stairs so as not to wake the kids and as I open the bedroom door ever so slowly, it creaks like a Hammer Horror film reminding me that I've got to get some WD40. I hear her move under the covers but she says nothing as I quickly undress, turn off the light and slip under the quilt. As my body touches hers I feel her stiffen.

"You're freezing" she mutters with a faraway tone.

"I know, I need warming up" I tell her as I wrap myself around her. Selfish I know but she feels so warm and enticing. Without warning my erection springs from nowhere and presses into the small of her back.

"*That's* not freezing" she says with a hint of mischief in her voice.

All of a sudden I'm consumed with passion and I caress her hips under my rapidly warming hands. She groans approval and reaches behind her to take me in her hand. As her fingers envelope me my entire body reacts as the blood courses through my veins like a tidal wave.

I sink my teeth gently into her neck and she lets out a low, guttural groan as I turn her over onto her back. In the gloom I can just about see her eyes beaming up at me, flooded with desire as I enter her, she arches her back and runs her nails over my skin as I penetrate her again and again.

Her hands run up the back of my neck onto my head and then it's all over.

The bedside light comes on to reveal a look of horror on my beloved's face.

"What's happened?" she demands as she inspects the large white dressing adorning my head.

"It's ok, don't worry" I tell her but it's far from enough and she goes into overdrive.

"It's ok?" she spits in disbelief "It's ok? Sammy, you've got a bloody big bandage stuck to the back of your head, how can it be ok?"

"Calm down babe, it's not as bad as it looks"

"Don't give me that rubbish, what happened?"

"Just a bit of trouble at the club that's all. It's just a bit of a scratch, looks worse than it is. I'm fine aren't I?"

The tears well up in her eyes.

"Come on babe, there's no need for that is there? I'm perfectly ok see?" I give her a daft look in the hope of bringing a smile to her face, I hate it when she cries, especially when I'm the cause.

It doesn't work and now she starts to cry.

"Oh Sammy, no amount of money can be worth this can it? Surely we can get by without it. I don't know how long I can stand this I really don't"

The last words are almost unrecognisable through her sobs.

Fucking hell don't do this to me *please.*

I go to take her in my arms but she pulls away.

"Come on babe, it's not that bad really. You know we need the money from the doors, even more so now as we've got another one on the way. It'd be financial suicide to pack it in now"

"What? As opposed to actual suicide dealing with lunatics who're going to hit you on the back of the head with...with...what did they hit you with?"

"A bottle I think but..."

"A bottle!? Bloody hell Sam, a bottle? What next hey? A knife? A gun? What next? A phone call from that monster of a boss to tell me you won't be coming home tonight because you've been killed like that poor lad in Widnes. He was killed for asking someone to put their hood down Sammy"

"I know babe, I know but..."

"But nothing Sammy, that's how easy it is nowadays isn't it? The scum out there don't give a toss that you've got a family that loves you and relies on you do they? Course they don't if they'll shoot you for asking them to take their hood down.

"Do you know what it's like for me every time you go out that door in that shirt and coat? It kills me Sammy it honestly does. Every time you shut the door I think it's going to be the last time I see you. I think about the kids growing up without their dad. Every time the phone rings while you're working I think it's going to be *the* call Sammy. The call to tell me you're not coming home ever again and I just can't stand it anymore Sammy, I can't" The last pleading words grate on my soul as again she falls into sobs.

Again I try to embrace her but again she pulls away.

"Come on Amy *please*" I beg as the emotion wells up in my own voice.

"Come here" I plead but she's adamant

"No Sammy" is all she says as she turns her back to me and cries into her pillow.

I lie down next to her and run my hands over my face. She'll be fine tomorrow, please god say she'll be fine tomorrow.

I know I won't sleep now. I never can do when she's upset.

Chapter 3

Sunday Morning eventually arrives and the light through the curtains illuminates her sleeping form.

She must have cried for an hour last night before she fell into a fitful sleep. Didn't get a wink myself.

I'm tired now though. Sickly tired.

This is going to be a hard day and I've got to work again tonight That's going to go down well an' all.

Maybe she'll have calmed down when she wakes up. Maybe things won't seem as bad in the cold light of day. Maybe this piercing headache will have subsided by tonight.

The little twat caught me good and proper there. Direct hit. The x-ray in the Royal last night confirmed that my skull wasn't fractured, but it feels like it's splitting open now. The pain is unbelievable and the meagre light poking through the gap in the curtain feels like laser beams burning my eyes out. Can't let her see I'm in pain though. I'll just nip downstairs for some paracetamol. That'll do the trick. That and a good hearty breakfast. Brilliant idea. I'll cook a fry up and serve it to her in bed with a smile, that should pacify her a little. Enough for me to get to work tonight at least.

As I make my way downstairs, every footfall sends shockwaves through my tortured head and I have to pause halfway down for the pain to settle and to steady myself.

My vision clears and I complete my epic journey to the bottom gingerly and carefully like I'm nursing the world's biggest hangover. That's really what it feels like, the mother of all hangovers and I realise that the day's going to be a lot worse than I first thought.

I shuffle into the kitchen, open the fridge and gaze at it's contents like old mother Hubbard. Not a strip of bacon dwells within it's frosty depths. Not much of anything dwells within it's frosty depths if I'm honest, save for a couple of cherry tomatoes and a lettuce that looks as though it's had it's day.

This means a trip to the shop. This means driving. This takes a moment of contemplation. Bollocks, the fresh air'll do me good.

The shop's only over the bridge but I take the car anyway. Can't face walking just yet.

I fly over and purchase the essentials as quickly as possible raising a few eyebrows of the local gossips with this huge white beacon stuck on the back of my loaf.

Back in the house, the smell of cooking bacon and sausages is tantalising in it's intensity and my stomach informs me that it's been too long since we last did business.

I get it all ready with the minimum of fuss and arrange the tray with various sauces, a large pot of fresh filter coffee and the small bunch of flowers, which I bought as an afterthought at the Spar.

Climbing the stairs I'm met with the vision that is my beautiful daughter standing on the landing.

"Hello Daddy" she beams. I swear to god she is image of her mother, absolutely dazzling.

"Good morning gorgeous. How's Daddy's little girl?"

"I'm okay" she replies matter of factly "Why was Mummy crying last night?"

Doesn't miss a trick this one. Straight to the point. She's only six but she has that manner that makes you think she's been here before.

"She was just a bit upset that's all sweetheart. She's fine now. What were you doing awake at that time anyway?"

"Oh I couldn't sleep"

Couldn't sleep? Six years old and she couldn't sleep.

"Is that a fact?" I say to her as I put the tray down and sweep her up in my arms. "And why was that?"

"I was worried about Paisley"

Paisley is our ageing cat who is sadly on his last legs. The arthritis in his hips has rendered him almost unable to move and even if he could, the cataracts covering his eyes would prevent him from seeing where he was going. The last visit to the vet's was a disturbing one after the whopper of a vet suggested that it would be better for Paisley if he put him to sleep. He imparted this pearl of wisdom in front of my distraught daughter. Needless to say the emotional fallout was devastating.

That was a week ago and the poor little fella is still struggling along and Molly barely lets him out of her sight, bless her.

"Molly love, Paisley is a very, very old cat. In cat years he'd be a hundred and ten at least and he's very sick"

"I know Daddy, I know but you're not going to let that nasty man put him to bed are you?"

"To sleep you mean sweetheart, to sleep. Not right now but there may come a time when it would be better for Paisley to go to cat heaven"

"Daddy, there's no such thing as cat heaven"

"And how do you know that?"

"Miss Turnbull in school said yesterday when I told her that our cat was sick"

"Oh she did, did she?" Bitter, twisted old cow. Fancy telling a distressed six year old that? "Well don't you listen to Miss Turnbull about things like that. You believe me don't you?"

"Yes Daddy but..."

"And have I ever lied to you before?"

"No Daddy" she says with a certain amount of resignation in her voice.

"No I haven't. and you know I'll do what's best for Paisley don't you?"

"Yes Daddy"

"Good girl now give me your biggest hug"

She throws her arms around my neck and almost squeezes the life out of me.

"I love you Daddy" she tells me from somewhere over my shoulder.

"I love you too sweetheart" I reply through the lump in my throat. So much for the big, hard doorman. Brought almost to tears by the compassion of my daughter.

"Now you go and look after your brother for me for a bit while I have a chat with your Mum"

"Okay Daddy" she says as I place her back on the floor and kiss her forehead. She truly is one amazing human being and the shear joy she brings me everyday is priceless. I dread the day when boys start to come knocking on the door I really do. It will take all my self-control to be somewhere near civil. And they will come. Nothing is surer. She is going to break some hearts and no mistake. That is a definite. No two ways about it. She is going to be a stunner, just like her mother.

I pick up the tray and creep into the bedroom. She's pretending to be asleep but I can tell from her breathing pattern that she's not.

I put the tray down on the bedside cabinet and placed my hand ever so gently on her shoulder. She flinches and moves away.

"Good morning sexy" I tell her in the hope of keeping things light hearted.

Slowly she turns round to face me, inspecting my face with a quizzical manner. After what seems like an eternity her stern expression melts a little.

"How's the head?" she enquires

"Fine" I lie "just a little fuzzy"

"Come here you daft sod" she sighs as she opens up her arms to embrace me and I go to her thankfully and hug her and envelope her and try to wrap my whole body around her. I hate it when she's upset. It hurts me so much it's almost physical. I kiss her neck and hold her as tight as I dare being ever mindful of the rapidly growing bump that signifies the imminent arrival of our third child.

I love the smell of her skin as it hit's the back of my nose and releases the residual tension, leaving me relaxed and relieved. This woman is amazing, more than that she is unique.

I lean back and gaze into her beautiful face.

"Fancy some brekky?" I ask as I motion towards the tray. She sees the flowers and her smile broadens.

"You didn't have to buy me flowers you big softy" she says, but I can tell from her face that she's glad I did.

And that's it, problem solved, panic over. Peace descends on the Jackson household once again until our breakfast in bed is vociferously interrupted by our four-year-old dynamo as he knocks vigorously on the door.

"Mummy, Daddy, are you awake yet!"

If we weren't already, we would be now.

"Come in" I tell him and he bounds through the door and onto the bed, grinning from ear to ear as he tries to throw his arms around the both of us at the same time. Molly follows close behind and there we all are, the nuclear family. 2 point 4 children.

CHAPTER 4

As I PARK MY CAR outside the Oak I can see Terry already standing in the doorway, grinning from ear to ear.

"Now then petal!" he shouts as I open the door and step out into the cold night air. I see his expression change as he spots the pad on the back of my head.

"Fuck's happened there kidder?" he enquires as I shake his hand in the customary manner.

"Vida's last night mate, fuckin' bedlam" And I relay the story of the bum fight at the lowlife corral.

"Who were they then?" Terry enquires as I finish the tale.

"No idea mate, H said he thought he recognised a couple of them from Bootle but he wasn't sure"

"Made a mess of them then?"

"H fuckin' did. One scary man when he gets going isn't he?"

"Fuckin' hell la isn't he, wouldn't like to be on the receiving end of that. How's your head?"

"Looks worse than it is. Just a few stitches and that. Blinding headache though"

"Did you get the cunt that bottled you?"

"Not sure, I hope so the fuckin' shitbag. If I didn't H certainly did"

Terry pulls a face of mock pain and we both laugh at the thought of the big monster on the rampage.

He's spot on Terry is. One hundred percent, all day and if I'm honest, I look forward to my Sunday nights on the Oak. It's generally quite quiet, touch wood, and we have a laugh. He's in a similar frame of mind as myself in as much as this is just a means to an end for him, just a job.

"Back in a mo' la" I tell him as I go inside to sign the book.

I re-emerge minutes later with two cans of Redbull and a flea in my ear from the manager.

"Napoleon's just given me down the banks about my headdress" I tell Terry.

"How d'you mean?"

"Said he didn't want me working in this condition"

"Cheeky twat, what did you say?"

"I told him to discuss it with H"

"Bet that shut him up"

"Oh aye" I confirm.

We pass an hour with idle chitchat and banter and then he hits me with it.

"How d'you fancy making a couple of grand?"

I give him a quizzical look.

"How?"

He then proceeds to tell me about a dealer who is offering us the names and addresses of his kilo men along with dates and times they'll be in alone. The deal is, we burst in, ballied up, relieve them of their stash, then sell the bugle back to the dealer for half bat. Apparently, we get to keep any cash that happens to be lying about the place as well. After making a few rapid calculations in my head I realise that we'd be in for a lot more than a couple of grand.

"So we're looking at twenty thousand each at least?"

"Give or take yeah. What d'you reckon?"

Twenty grand could really bail us out of the shit at this precise moment in time I don't mind saying.

"Fuckin' hell Terry lad, it's a bit severe isn't it?"

16

"Yeah and no" he replies "We'd be in and out, no messin' an' who the fuck's gonna suspect us eh?"

"What about this dealer?"

"He's solid la. Hundred and ten percent. No-one's gonna suspect him either. It's fool proof mate and not bad odds for an evening's work"

He's only right. Twenty bag of sand for robbing a few scumbags is extremely good money.

"So we're just gonna' charge in there, screamin' and rantin'?" I enquire

"Yep" he replies, grinning like the proverbial Cheshire cat

"And what if they don't want to hand over the goods?"

"They aren't gonna' have a choice la. Who's gonna' argue with a piece stuck in their face?"

"Ah" there it is. The point where I should say thanks but no thanks. The point where I should change the conversation and forget about twenty thousand pounds. But I don't.

"Where's the gun comin' from" I ask somewhat warily.

"Jerry Jacobs" he informs me. This is getting worse "We can borrow it and we only have to pay for it if we use it"

"So we can just hand it back for nothing?"

"Yeah, dead easy. What d'you reckon?"

This takes a moment's contemplation, but only a moment.

"When?" Is the only question that comes to mind.

"Wednesday night all being well"

"Fuck it, why not?"

CHAPTER 5

I FUCKIN' HATE LYING TO her, I really do. It's not something I'm good at and doesn't she know it. I look guilty even when I'm not. Have done ever since I was a nipper. I remember in assemblies in school when the headmaster would announce that someone's bag had been stolen from the cloakroom and the culprit would make life easier on his or herself if they came clean, I would always cherry up even though it had fuck all to do with me.

I've been searched in every major airport I've ever been to. Strip searched in some cases which is not the most pleasant of experiences I can tell you.

I've just got one of those faces. Guilty as sin.

Thing is, she can read me like a book. And when I say book, I'm talking Spot the Dog, not War and Peace. She knows me far too well, so this is going to have to be a performance worthy of an Oscar nomination. I'm going to have to be Gary Oldman, or DeNiro. I'm going to have to get into the part, method acting if you will. I'm going to have to convince myself that I'm working on Wednesday night. That's all there is to it. I'm working on Wednesday night. I am working on Wednesday night. I am working at the Oak on Wednesday night. I am working at the Oak, with Terry on Wednesday night. I'm fucked basically. I couldn't convince an alchy to let me buy him a pint. I couldn't sell a burger to a starving man.

I fucking hate lying to her, I really do.

CHAPTER 6

I THINK SHE'S GONE FOR it. I think she actually believes me! I've just left the house and as far as I can tell, she's fine with it. No questions asked, no looks of suspicion, just the usual kiss for her and the kids and away I went. Like clockwork. Dead fuckin' easy. Move over Bobby lad, Sammy Jackson is the new king of the silver screen. That was worthy of a Nobel Prize never mind an Oscar.

I'm in the car, away over the bridge and down Bold Lane. The stereo's on and Bad Moon Rising is blasting out from Clog FM.

> Don't go round tonight,
> Cos' it's bound to take your life,
> There's a bad moon on the rise.

John Fogarty's immortal voice screams out the lyrics as if he's trying to warn me to give tonight a miss. Not what you want to hear when you're on your way to do something like this.

I change the station and get 'Should have known better' by Jim Diamond. For fuck's sake!

I turn off the radio and try to turn my thoughts about the job in hand into something positive.

They're only scumbags after all. Peddlers of misery and empty dreams and if I'm perfectly honest, I couldn't give a toss about any of them. I've got no qualms about poking a shooter in their grids and taking whatever we can off've them. That's not the problem. That's a piece of piss.

No, it's getting in and out unseen that's concerning me. We can't exactly stroll down the path with balaclavas over our heads now can we? Whatever will the neighbours think? And the last thing we need is a fucking vigilante storming in and complicating matters now isn't it?

I'm sure Terry has it all in hand but I can't relax until I know the details, until everything's boxed off and squared away. It's just the way I am. Got to cover every angle. Got to dot the i's and cross the t's. Got to be one hundred percent sure before I can settle.

My nerves are jangling now if I'm perfectly honest and it's taking a large amount of concentration to keep my mind on the road.

I see the red light at Maghull traffic lights just in time and the car screeches to a halt next to a rather alarmed looking pensioner in a Rover.

Fuckin' calm down Sammy lad, ease up. It'll be fine and in a few hours you're gonna be quite a few grand in the black. Just think about what you can do with the dough and how it's going to make life easier for all concerned.

Switch Island is virtually empty and I sail through well within the speed limit. Don't want to attract any unwanted attention now do I?

Past the Asda, then the Old Roan and onwards past the Black Bull and through Orrell Park.

Just before the Queens Drive roundabout, I pull into a side road, park up and walk up to the Black Horse.

Terry's sitting there on his own in a corner, sipping on a Blackcurrant and Lemmo. On seeing me a grin splits his face and he raises his glass.

"Now then flower"

Chapter 7

THE FIRST ONE, IT TURNS out, is cushy. Nice secluded cul-de-sac, easy access to the back garden, minimal visibility at the front door. Perfect.

We're in and out before the poor fucker even realises what's going on. So now we're travelling down Queens Drive with a kilo of bugle and just over five grand in cash in a cloned Subaru Legacy courtesy of Terrence. He'd had the plates made last week and robbed the car last night. The owner of the genuine car, a Mr Ronald Brown, would have no idea that a carbon copy of his pride and joy is cruising the streets of Liverpool tonight. Terry had actually gone through the fella's rubbish to find out his details before he'd had the plates made. Talk about thorough.

He couldn't have picked a better car for the job. Discreet, anonymous and fucking rapid. Just the job.

We pull into the road of the next victim and it becomes all too apparent that this one's not so simple.

There's kids everywhere, playing football and riding bikes and generally being everywhere all at once. Terry points out the house in question and it's right in view of the whole street. Not good.

We drive by being casually observed by some of the more inquisitive little urchins and turn out of the street.

Terry parks the car a few streets away and we stroll back.

"We're both gonna have to go through the back door on this one" Terry advises "I saw a jigger at the end of the street which should lead to the back garden"

"What if he makes it to the front door?" I enquire

"We're just gonna have to be fuckin' quick la. Here y'are" he says as he passes me the pistol "You can have the shooter this time"

"Sound" is all I can think of to say as I feel it's weight in my hand.

"I told JJ that we wanted a revolver but he's given us this" Terry says as he gestures towards the nine millimetre automatic.

"Why did we want a revolver?" I enquire somewhat blankly.

"If we have to fire it a revolver doesn't leave any cartridges does it? I'm fucked if I'm going to go scrabbling around on me hands and knees lookin' for a casing that's probably rolled under the settee, know what I mean?"

He's got a point. I can't be certain but I'm getting the feeling that this isn't the first time he's done something like this. Seems to have all angles covered does our Terrance. Not that I'm complaining of course. On the contrary, his professionalism is boosting my own confidence no end.

I tuck the gun into the waste band of my jeans for no other reason than that's how I've seen it done in the films and close my coat around me.

The alleyway does indeed lead to the next lucky punter's back garden, although it takes us a few minutes to work out which house is his from the back. Don't want to go charging into some poor unfortunate soul's abode, waving a shooter in his face and demanding drugs when we've got the wrong house now do we? Definitely not PC.

As we vault the fence I can feel the silencer digging into my upper thigh as a stark reminder of the severity of our actions. What the fuck am I doing? Reality hits me ever so briefly as we approach the house and the try the back door. He's only gone and left it open hasn't he the soft twat.

Without hesitation, we're in and running for him before he has time to make it to the front door. He has no chance. Looks half stoned to be honest and he goes down like a sack of shit.

I pull the pistol from my kecks, point it straight into his face and give it my best cockney accent.

"Where is it?"

"Where's what?" he replies terror running wild over his dial.

"You know what, the fackin' Charlie" Charlie? Who the fuck calls it Charlie nowadays?

"I haven't got none" he lies instinctively.

I shove the pistol deep within his mouth and ask again.

"Where is it?"

His eyes roll back in his head like pinballs as a dark stain spreads across the front of his jeans.

"Mmmmmph!" he protests around the sides of the silencer. I take it out so he can speak.

"Yes?" I enquire.

"It's in the cupboard!" he blurts as he points to the kitchen. Dead Fuckin' Easy.

Terry goes over, pulls out the bag of pure white powder, places it in the rucksack on my back and pulls out the duck tape.

Minutes later our victim is encased like a mummy and we're rummaging through his gaff.

I open one cupboard to find a box of nine millimetre shells and for some reason, I slip a couple into my pocket.

"Where's your dosh?" I ask, still keeping up the cockney accent to the best of my ability.

"I 'aven't got any" he lies "I've given it all for that lot"

I move towards him to place the gun back in his mouth and he bottles it.

"Ok! Ok!" he rapidly concedes "Behind the vinyl"

Terry saunters over to his vast record collection and goes to start pulling them off the shelf.

"Woe! Woe! Bottom shelf, behind the Zeppelin" he panics.

Terry pulls out ten albums and his eyes light up. Without saying a word he brings over the bundle of cash and at a quick guesstimate I see that it's a fair amount.

"Very fackin' nice" I tell him "Very nice indeed. Now then, if we find out you've tried to get up and alert anyone in the next hour, we're gonna come back and plug you, comprende?"

Our victim nods his head vigorously.

"Good boy" I turn to Terry "Well kimosabe, our work here is done. Shall we depart?" Even through the balaclava I can see his grin.

"Chocks away Ginger!" and we're out of there.

CHAPTER 8

THE THIRD ONE SAILS BY and before I know it, we're at the main dealer's abode, standing in his front room with a rucksack full of beak.

"You got all three then?"

"Yep" Terry replies "No bother"

"Very good lads, very good. Have the parcels been opened?"

"No they're all still sealed" Terry says. Terry can do all the talking as far as I'm concerned. We're at the finishing post now and I can feel a sense of elation flowing over me. That was too fuckin' easy.

"Let's have a look then" the juicehead says as he motions for Terry to pass him the bag.

"You've got our money then?" Terry enquires as he hands it over.

"Kind of la, yeah, kind of" he replies distractedly.

"What do you mean kind of?" I interject. Something in the lad's tone has struck a chord in me and I can't help my inquisitiveness.

"Well lads. Seein' as you made a very tidy profit from the surplus cash lying around the place, I'm only gonna' give you sevens"

"You fuckin' what?" Terry spits incredulously.

"You heard me la. Seven grand a key and that's generous"

"And what's to stop us takin' the gear elsewhere?" Terry asks.

"Me" says the grock as he stands and squares up to Terry.

26

Before I realise what I'm doing, the pistol is out of my waste band and in the prick's face.

"Sit down big man" I tell him as he smiles at me with over confidence.

"And what the fuck are you gonna' do with that knobhead?"

"You're starting to get my dander up you grotty little man" I've always wanted to use that line. Heard it on Fawlty Towers years ago.

The grock's confidence wavers a little as he tries to ascertain what he's up against.

"Terry, take the bag off've him" a quick glance at Terry tells me that he's not entirely au fait with the situation, but he does as I ask all the same.

"Where's our dough?"

"Fuck off!"

I hear the report of the gun before I realise I've pulled the trigger. Then silence descends upon the room for what seems like an eternity.

"What the fuck...?" Terry's voice eventually splits the peace and I turn to look at him, then back to the grock. Judging from his vacant stare I must've hit him square in the heart.

"It was him or us la"

"Do you know who that was?" he asks me somewhat blankly.

"No, who?"

"Jamie Buck? Billy Buck's nephew"

"And..."

"And? Fuckin' and? Jesus Christ la you've just plugged Billy Buck's nephew!"

"Does he know about it?"

"No but..."

"And is he gonna find out?"

"Well no, but..."

"Well there's nothing to panic about then is there?"

"Fuckin' hell la this is bad, this is very bad"

27

"Listen, did anyone other than this prick know that we was doin' this job tonight?"

"No"

"You sure?"

"Yeah, he's not gonna go advertisin' the fact that he's bumpin' his own dealers is he?"

"We're in the clear then aren't we?"

"I suppose so"

"Fuckin' right we are. Now lets not waste any time here. There's at least twenty one grand sittin' around here somewhere, plus god knows what else so let's get busy, eh?"

"Yeah" is all Terry can say.

After twenty minutes of frantic searching, we sit at the table and survey our haul.

There's our original three kilos, plus another four that we've unearthed, plus at least fifty thousand in used notes. Fuckin' bingo!

"We're gonna' need another bag" I suggest as I scale the stairs four at a time. I'm into one bedroom but there's fuck all there. Into the next and I'm brought to an abrupt halt by the sight that confronts me.

Lying on the bed, arm festooned by a tourniquet and a dangling syringe, is a girl of no more than seventeen. She's absolutely out of it and blissfully unaware of the carnage that's gone on downstairs.

Next to the bed is a Head bag and when I look inside I see packets of brown powder.

Naughty, naughty. This steg head must've been dabbling in a bit of the other as well. Very un-PC. Just not cricket.

I grab the bag, bolt back downstairs and fill it to the brim with the rest of the booty. I don't tell Terry about sleeping beauty.

"This is a detached house isn't it?" I ask Terry.

"Yeah, why?"

Without replying I open the oven, turn it and all the gas rings on and stuff a newspaper into the toaster and push the button down.

"I saw this one in a film"

"What the fuck are you doin'?" Terry asks incredulously.

"Our dabs and DNA are all over this place la and we need to cover our tracks, get me?"

"For fuck's sake!" Terry exclaims as we both bolt for the back door and over the back fence.

We don't get far before the dull bang rocks the neighbourhood, quickly followed by numerous car alarms and barking dogs.

"Walk la, just walk. We can't run or people will notice"

"Yeah Ok" Terry replies but I can see he's as eager as me to burst into a sprint.

We'd parked the car a few streets away as a matter of course and now it seems like miles. There's all kinds of mayhem going on and here's me and T, ambling along the street in the opposite direction with a bag each. The urge to get to the car is almost unbearable.

We eventually reach it and place the bags in the boot. Once inside, Terry guns the engine and we drift out of the disaster area, hopefully unnoticed.

Neither of us utters a word until we're back on Queens Drive.

"Right then" I pipe up "What the fuck are we gonna do with all this shit now?"

"I've got a flat on Breck Road that nobody knows about" Terry replies "We'll sort it all out there"

Why Terrance my old chum, you dark horse you...

Chapter 9

THE FLAT IS SPARSE TO say the least. Some heavyset curtains and a few sticks of furniture and that's it.

The swag is sitting on the rickety table in the middle of the room and we set about dividing up the money. It works out at just over thirty five thousand pounds each, which I'm sure you'll agree, is not bad for a night's work.

"Where the fuck are we gonna get rid of seven Kilos of bugle?" I enquire.

"Don't worry about that la" says Terry, his composure fully regained "I know a fella"

"Not in the city?"

"No la, from far, far away this kid. We'll have to set up a meetin' next week. Shouldn't be a problem"

"What price do you reckon we'll get?"

"Twenty two's easy"

A quick mental calculation puts a smile on my face.

"That's a hundred and fifty four thousand notes"

"At least"

"Fuckin' hell la" the full extent of the value of the gear hadn't registered with me until now.

"And what about this?" I ask as I pull the bags of brown from the head bag. Terry's face drops.

"Where did you get those?"

"They were in the bag when I found it"

"That's naughty that la, that's very naughty indeed. The Buck's are pedallin' smack now? This is very useful information this is"

"Who the fuck are we gonna' tell?" I enquire.

"No-one mate, just good to know these things isn't it?" he replies with a smile.

"We need to get rid of all our clobber and the motor" I suggest as Terry stashes the last of the bags under the loose floorboards he's pulled up.

"No problems kidder, I know just the place"

CHAPTER 10

WE STAND AND WATCH A while as the flames take hold. There's no chance we'll be seen here. Not at this time of night. Got to make sure it all goes up though. Can't leave anything incriminating. Got to cover all tracks.

"There's only one more problem to take care of now la" Terry says as he turns to look at me.

"And that is?"

"The shooter. JJ's gonna' know we've fired it cos it'll 'ave one bullet missin' won't it?"

I just smile and pull a nine-millimetre shell from the pocket of my clean trousers.

"Where the fuck did you get that?"

"That second job. He had a box of them in his cupboard so I thought it'd be too good an opportunity to miss"

"How's that like?"

"Well I replaced the bullet in the chamber with a new one so if forensics get on the case, they'll find it matches the ones in that prick's house"

"Very nice la, very fuckin' nice. How'd you know there'd be trouble?"

"I didn't. Just better safe than sorry"

"Happy days! No-one'll miss the big juice head anyway, the fuckin' bully. Not a very popular lad truth be known"

"I must admit I didn't take to him"

We both fall into fits of giggles fuelled by nervous tension and relief. But behind the laughter I'm wondering if the seventeen year old heroin user will be missed. I think of my own daughter. No matter what she got into I'd still adore her all the same. Nothing she could do could change my feelings for her one iota. Will a distraught father be getting the worse possible news from plod tomorrow morning? Will a family be coming to terms with the loss of one so dear? Will a community be shocked at the departure of one of it's own?

She wouldn't have felt a thing, judging from the state of her. I hope she didn't feel a thing. I really, really hope that the smack had it's desired effect as an analgesic and kept her unconscious and unaware of the breakdown of her body.

Terry's still chuckling, Blissfully unaware of the secondary piece of this mess. Ignorance, it would seem, is actually bliss. He's happy as a sandboy.

We've a long walk back to town before we can even think about using any form of transport and I suggest we get going.

"Right you are then" Terry replies with a spring in his step "Turned out nice again!"

If only...

33

CHAPTER 11

BACK AT TERRY'S FLAT, WE both scrub ourselves down with petrol to remove any traces from our bodies and Terry has first shower to wash off the residue. I sit on the rickety chair at the unstable table and the magnitude of what I've just done hits me like a cannon. This is the first chance I've had since all this madness started to actually take stock of the situation and the situation is this; I am a murderer. I have taken not only one life but two. One of which, you might possibly argue, deserved what he got. But the other one, the seventeen year old girl lying on a bed upstairs, guilty of nothing more than being in the wrong place at the wrong time, did she deserve it? Did she deserve to have her life cut short for no other reason than convenience?

I can't believe how quickly I made the decision to do this as well. I'd shot the steg head before I even thought about it. It was more of a reaction than anything else. Truth be known I didn't exactly like the fella but fuckin' shooting him? How the fuck did I get to that? I'm a family man. In the daytime I have a very responsible, very respectable job. I am not a gangster. I am not a bully. I shouldn't actually be a fuckin' doorman but needs must.

That brings us to the girl. I can't get her face out of my mind. She looked so serene, so peaceful. Granted her euphoria was brought on with the aid of the poppy, but fuckin' hell. What have I done? How could I make the decision to end her life so easily? And I did.

34

Without much deliberation I chose to torch the house with her inside just to tie everything up. Just to ensure our safety, liberty and continued life. I wonder if she woke up before the end? I wonder if her last dying moments were spent in agonising pain as the flames tore the flesh from her body. I wonder if at the end she was actually aware that she was dying?

The horror of my actions mixed with the stench of the petrol prove too much and my stomach gives way as I lurch towards the kitchen sink and redecorate the stained porcelain in a glorious shade of vomitus as the entire contents of my guts surge forward uncontrollably.

When the retching finally subsides, I turn on the taps and hastily clean the bowl. Can't show any signs of weakness.

Plonking myself back down on the chair I feel empty, gutted, wretched. My mind is spinning frenziedly as I struggle to gain control of my thoughts. Can't let Terry see me like this. Got to regain my composure. Got to get a grip. My children's faces burst into my head and the guilt I feel explodes. How could I let them down? How could I do something so heinous when they rely on me and love me? How can I go back and be the same Daddy when I've done something like this? The tears well up in the corners of my eyes and I fight to keep them back.

Then, last but by no means least, Amy's beautiful countenance glides up before my eyes and the tears flow unchecked. I've let her down. I've let her down so badly that I'm not sure there's any way back. How can I look her in the eyes again? She'll see. Of that I'm sure. She'll see something's wrong. She knows me only too well and she'll know there's something badly out of place. She can read me, she knows me better than I know myself. How can I hide this from her? Panic grips me like a vice. I am fucked.

Terry pops his head round the door.

"Your turn la. What's up with your eyes?"

"Eh?" I utter, desperately trying to pull myself together "Oh, just got some petrol in them that's all" I say as I grab my towel and go into the bathroom to cleanse myself.

The water feels good against my skin and I scrub vigorously to remove the stench of petrol and the events of the night. I must admit the action of bathing is soothing my stricken mind. Taking away at least some of the feeling of filth from myself, although the reek of petrol is still strong and I scour away at my body, desperate to remove all trace of the night's activities.

After what seems like a lifetime, I eventually turn off the water and towel myself down. Quickly dressing in my clean, original clothes, I make my way back out to the front room where Terry is enjoying a large Jack Daniels.

"It's just been on the news" he informs me "House fire in West Derby, Police aren't ruling out foul play"

My stomach leaps. Pretty soon they're going to announce that there was two bodies found and that's going to raise some serious questions from my partner in crime.

"Did they say anything else?" I ask a little too nonchalantly.

"No, just that there's Police and fire crew at the scene. There's nothing to link us though is there? Even if the car was caught on camera, it's fuckin' toast now isn't it?"

"Yeah" is all I can say.

"It's fuckin' happy days then isn't it?" Terry chirps a little too happily "Home and hosed, literally"

"Is right"

CHAPTER 12

AS PER USUAL THE BEDSIDE light is on and as per usual she's pretending to be asleep. I quickly undress, slide in behind her and flick the light off.

"Why do you smell of petrol?" she asks straight out of the blue.

"Eh?" I reply, stalling for time, desperately trying to think my way out of a very sticky situation. Can't believe I haven't thought about this before.

"I can smell petrol Sam"

"Oh that? Terry's car ran out so we had to get some from the garage. Tried filling one of those petrol cans up and it went everywhere"

"Oh" she replies distantly. Close la, very fuckin' close.

I snuggle in to the back of her neck and kiss her just behind the ear, but she's already asleep. I can tell by the tone of her breathing. Safe for tonight but bizarrely half of me wants her to stay awake. Half of me wants her to stay with me, to comfort me, to soothe me, to reassure me.

As I lie here in the dark, my conscience does it's best to kick the shit out of me as the pains in my empty stomach escalate to an almost unbearable level.

What have I done? Jesus Christ, what have I done?

There will be no sleep tonight. Not a chance. Not a hope in hell and all I can do is lie here for the next five hours and let my mind torture me. I have never looked forward to a sunrise so much in my life.

CHAPTER 13

I'M UP BEFORE THE ALARM and into the shower, scrubbing away to try to completely remove any traces of the au de gasoline.

After about twenty minutes I'm more or less convinced that I'm odour free and I dry myself off and rapidly get dressed.

I need to get out of the house as soon as possible. Need to be away from here so I can gather my thoughts and start to come terms with all that's gone on.

Amy'll see to the kids. Got to get out. I feel like a teenager sneaking out of the house before his parents collar him for the previous night's mischief.

Panic starts to well up in my chest. If she sees me this morning she'll know there's something up. The look on my face, I can only imagine, would get me hung.

I've got to go in and give her a kiss though. If I don't, she'll definitely know there's something up. Please god say she's still asleep.

The door creaks again as I go back in the bedroom. Fuckin' WD40! How many times do I have to remind myself? Fuckin' WD40. Today I will get some. No excuses.

She's lying with her back to me. Motionless. I lean over a kiss the back of her head.

"You're going in early aren't you?" she enquires.

"I know, I've got a meeting at nine and I need to sort a few things out"

"Drive carefully"

And I'm out of there.

CHAPTER 14

No SOONER AM I OUT of our road than my mobile rings. Looking at the screen I see it's Terry. I know full well what this'll be about. I haven't heard the news this morning but I'm positive I know what it's content will have been.

I push the green button and put the phone reluctantly to my ear.

"Now then petal"

"We need to talk" Terry replies in a 'this is serious shit' tone of voice.

"Meet me in the office in an hour" I tell him.

The phone goes dead in my hand.

CHAPTER 15

The intrusive sound of the buzzer jogs me from my thoughts and makes me jump. I pick up the intercom phone.

"Hello, LIFT, can I help you?"

"It's me"

I press the front door release button and replace the handset.

Minutes later the office door opens and in marches a more than slightly perplexed Terry.

"Two bodies la" is all he has to say.

I haven't got the energy, inclination or ability to act well enough to carry off a bluff.

"I know"

"A fifteen year old girl la, fifteen for fuck's sake!"

"I know" Fifteen? Fuckin' hell she didn't look that young last night I swear to god. But would it have made a difference if she had?

"Did you see her?"

"What?" I reply, stalling for time.

"Last night, when you went upstairs for that bag, did you see her?"

Shit or bust time now. Do I lie and feign ignorance or do I just come clean? Fuck it, in for a penny…

"Yeah la, I did"

"What?" comes Terry's incredulous reply.

"She was smacked off her face, lyin' on a bed with a needle hangin' out of her arm"

Terry's sense of shock is as clear as day as this latest piece of news rocks him to his foundations. He really didn't expect this.

"You're not serious?"

"Deadly"

"So you just torched the place knowin' full well that she was upstairs?"

"Yep" I reply a little too coldly.

"Fuckin' hell la are you sick or what? She was only fifteen for fuck's sake! Fifteen!"

"She looked older" is all I can think of to say.

"You fuckin' what?"

"Honestly, she looked older"

"And that makes a difference does it?"

"Not really la no. Look I dealt with a situation that was beyond our control right? Once the grock was shot we had no choice"

"You shouldn't even have shot him though should you?" Terry protests.

"And you'd've been happy with sevens would you?"

"No but..."

"But fuck all la! He deserved what he got and if we didn't do it some other fucker would've. That left us with a situation though didn't it? It was all unavoidable. How could we 'ave kept her alive? Dragged her out and took her with us? Just wasn't goin' to happen was it?"

"No" Terry concedes.

"I didn't tell you about her last night cos' we had enough on our plate with all the rest of it, get me?"

"Yeah"

"Fuckin' right yeah. What's done's done though. There's no goin' back, so we've just got to move on right?"

"I suppose"

"There's no suppose about it. What else did they say on the news?"

"Not a lot, foul play, possible arson attack, a bit cagey really"

"Good, that means they've got fuck all. Keep our heads down and we're laughin'"

Terry's still unsure though. I can see it written all over his grid and this concerns me. Don't be the weak link in the chain Terry lad for god's sake. Let's stick together on this and we'll get through unscathed. Solidarity brother.

"Have you had a word with your contacts about the gear yet?"

"Phoned him this mornin'" he replies, glad of a change of subject "We're on for next Monday"

"Where?"

"Keswick"

"Keswick? In the Lakes?"

"Yeah, I said it was out of town didn't I?"

"Yeah but fuckin' Keswick? Who's gonna' want a shedfull of bugle in Keswick?"

"You'd be surprised?" Terry smiles.

This is going to involve more lies to Amy and this makes me just that little bit more unsure. Should I just tell Terry that the gear's his and wash my hands of the whole matter? Walk away and be happy with the sizeable amount of cash I've already made? Fuck that. There's another seventy odd grand to be had here and that would most definitely make life more than comfortable.

"When're we going up then?" I ask.

"Sunday night'd be best. We can 'ave a few pints if we get there early enough"

"Sounds good" This gets worse. More lies. How the fuck am I going to explain this one? An overnight stay? Not good. Not good at all.

CHAPTER 16

THE DAYS PASS BY AND every knock at the door sends me into a blind panic. But no police come to call.

The family of the fifteen year old girl make an emotional plea on television for anyone with any information to come forward, but no-one does.

The question has occurred to me that what was Jamie Buck doing with a fifteen year old girl in his gaff? She was no relation to him so what was he doing? It would appear that not only was he an arrogant, conceited bully, but he was also a fuckin' kiddie fiddler as well. A dirty, filthy, scummy beast that preyed on young girls. It would appear that I have done the world a favour and this rationale makes me feel, in an ever so tiny way, that much better.

I've told Amy that I've got to go and see a client in Keswick which is not entirely lying is it? I've told her that I'm going up on the Sunday evening so as to get an early start on the Monday morning and she's gone for it. Either she's not as perceptive as I've given her credit for, or I'm an amazing actor. Neither of which are in any way plausible. Can't make her out at the mo'. Can't read her at all. Oh well, no news is good news eh?

Big H wasn't very happy when I rung him and told him I need Sunday off, especially as Terry had rung him only hours before with the same request, but fuck him. With a bit of luck and a bit of good management, I won't be on the doors for very much longer.

CHAPTER 17

I PICK TERRY UP AT six and I must admit, this has a lad's on the lash feel about it. The fact that we've got enough class A in the boot to put us away for the next twenty years seems to be immaterial.

Terry's in his usual fine spirits and the banter flows back and forth for most of the journey. The roads are pretty clear and before we know it we're driving through Keswick town centre.

"Any ideas?" Terry enquires when I mention accommodation.

"Yeah, head towards Stonethwaite, I know just the place"

The Langstrath Arms is a beautifully secluded hotel in the heart of Borrowdale. I know I sound like Judith Chalmers here, but it's true. I used to come to the campsite further down the valley when I was a kid and the area has always had a certain magic for me.

As it happens there is a twin room available and after checking in and dumping the bags, not to mention the precious cargo, we retire to the bar to sip on a long, cool, pint whilst relaxing by the blazing log fire.

It's difficult to believe that we're here to do a drug deal. I haven't felt so relaxed in months. I fuckin' love this place.

Terry's on form as well, getting the barmaid's number within the space of an hour. Typical.

We then take a walk to the Borrowdale Arms and join in with the walkers, climbers and fell runners in getting completely and absolutely pissed.

Terry's blagging this curvaceous young outdoor fanatic that he's done the three peaks in record time, but he comes unstuck, when he can't actually put a name to any of them. He carry's on regardless though and succeeds in getting her number as well. Smarmy sod.

We eventually fall back into the hotel at sometime after two and the next thing I know, I'm being rudely awoken by the shrill of the alarm on my phone. I stare at the screen through bleary eyes to see that it's seven thirty. Time to get up for a hearty breakfast. This just gets better.

I don't suffer from hangovers as a rule but Terry's a little worse for wear.

"Now then kidder, wakey, wakey"

Terry just murmurs and shifts under his duvet.

"Come on now petal, things to do, people to see!"

"Yeah, yeah, give us a minute" He grunts from somewhere under the covers.

"Not feeling to chipper?"

"Fuck off"

"Charming"

I dive in the shower, have a quick shave and get dressed, ready to face the day. Despite the agenda, I'm feeling on top of the world, a million dollars and I can't quite work out why.

The breakfast is indeed fantastic. The full works, Sausage, bacon, two fried eggs, mushrooms, fried slice, black pudding, a mountain of toast and plum tomatoes. It has to be plum tomatoes on a fry up. Fresh grilled just don't cut the mustard.

I wolf mine down and am delighted when our congenial host brings me second helpings. This is livin'! Terry's struggling with his and looks a little green around the gills.

"Come on now flower, breakfast is the most important meal of the day" I tell him.

"Mmmph" he replies through a mouthful of toast.

"What time is this fella expecting us?"

Terry washes his toast down with a mouthful of tea "Nine"

"Do you know where it is?"

"Oh aye, dead fuckin' easy"

"And he's a big player then is he?"

"How d'you mean?"

"Well" I reduce my voice to a whisper so as to keep our conversation from the rest of the dining room, "He's taking seven keys off us with money up front so he's got to have a bit of clout hasn't he?"

"Oh aye. Big hitter in these parts is Rodney"

"Rodney?"

"Yeah, that's our man. He's all day la. No problems"

"If he's that big in these parts what's to say he's not bein' watched?"

"By who?"

"Jeremy Beadle, who'd you think? The bizzies"

"No way la. He's too shrewd for all that caper. No worries there. He's water tight. He's got half the plod around here in his pocket anyway"

"Yeah?"

"Fuckin' right la. Don't be worryin' about all that. Safe as houses"

That'll do for me. Time to stop worrying and get on with the day.

CHAPTER 18

THE JOURNEY BACK TO KESWICK is spectacular with Derwent Water stretched out to our left and the fells and cliffs to our right. It was pitch black when we arrived last night and until now, I'd forgotten just how amazing the scenery around here is. The road is spot on as well and the Golf GTi is eating up the bends. I'm slightly disappointed when we eventually arrive in Keswick to be honest.

The house is conveniently situated on the outskirts of the town and we're there and inside within minutes.

Terry and Rodney shake hands like old friends and Terry turns to introduce me.

"Rodney this is Sammy I told you about"

"Alroight buddy" he says in a thick Brummie accent as he extends a hand in greeting.

"Now then" I reply as we shake. This fella must stick out like a spare prick at a wedding around here with that dialect.

"Youm come up last noight then?" he enquires.

"Yeah" Terry replies "Thought we'd sample some local hospitality and that"

"Very noice, very noice. Yow got the gear then?"

"Same old Rodney eh? Straight down to business?"

"Yow know me Tirroye. I loike to 'ave things stitched up sharpish loike"

"Suits me Rodders" Terry says with a smile as he produces the seven white bags from the rucksack.

"Youm don't moind if oi take a sample for testing do yow?"

"Not at all Rodney, not at all" Terry's hangover seems to have dissipated and he is now in full flow, taking on the role with gusto and verve.

Rodney makes a small incision in one of the bags, removes a sample on a spatula and drops it into an awaiting test tube. After swilling it around for a couple of seconds his eyes light up.

"Bloimey! This is good stuff this is Tirrance. Very good stuff indeed. What are yow looking for? Proice woise that is?"

"What are you payin' up here?"

"Ah, that's not the question though is it? The question is how much do yow want to take this off your 'ands roight now"

"Make us an offer" says Terry, obviously enjoying the banter.

"How about twenty foives?"

I have to stifle a cough and stop myself from reacting. Twenty fives! Overall that's twenty one grand more than we were expecting! Happy... Fuckin'... Days!

Terry takes it all in his stride.

"I think twenty six would be nearer the mark, don't you?"

"Yow droive a hard bargain yow do Tirroye, twenty six it is then"

My heart nearly leaps up into my mouth. Twenty six per kilo that's, one hundred and eighty two thousand pounds! I'll just repeat that for effect. One hundred and eighty two thousand pounds! Split two ways it's ninety one grand each. Added to the thirty five I've already got, it's one hundred and twenty six big ones. It's all I can do to contain my joy and my resolve is tested further when Rodney opens up a large case and starts counting out the dough in bundles of five grand.

"You know oi would've gone to twenty seven for gear this good lads"

"Never mind Rodney me old mucker, never mind. Have the other seven on us" Terry cheerfully informs him as we fill our own bags with the cash.

This is just too fucking simple. Far too simple. What kind of fella carries this amount of wedge with him? The way he's dealing it out you'd think it was toffee. The bag from which he's drawing the dosh is rammed and the thought flits across my mind that maybe we should relieve him of it. Crackers I know, but I can't deny the fact that I'm thinking about fleecing this magnificent benefactor stood before us. Terry doesn't know, but I've brought the shooter with me just in case. Well, you never know do you? Not after the last time. Don't want some smarmy twat trying to take us for a ride again now do we? But this fella is far from smarmy. I quite like the lad to be perfectly honest. There's none of that 'I am a moody gangster' shit. Just a nice, daft, Brummie on the make and good luck to him. Of course I'm not going to have him over. Not my style is it? Can't deny I thought about it though. Where the fuck did that come from?

"We right then kidder?" Terry snaps me back from my thoughts.

"Eh?"

"We ready for the off?"

"Oh, yeah, nice one"

"Rodney, it's been a pleasure as always"

"Loikewise, Tirrance, always good to do business with you Scousers, don't get all that bollocks that you get from the Cockneys"

"We're all day us kidder that's why. One hundred and ten percent professional and we know a good deal when we see one"

"Let's not get carried away" Rodney jokes and we all chuckle.

After a brief round of handshaking, we're out of there.

CHAPTER 19

THE JOURNEY HOME IS A joyful one and the relief that we're no longer carrying twenty years in jail in the boot is magnificent.

My mobile rings in my pocket and when I look at the screen I see that it's Amy. I put my finger to my mouth to tell Terry to be quiet and push the green button.

"Hello sexy"

"Hello you, how did it go?"

"Fantastic babe, absolutely fantastic. If we clinch this deal it's gonna mean a hefty bonus for yours truly"

"Seriously?"

"Oh aye girl. This is worth a fortune. Should know for definite midweek"

"Oh Sammy that's wonderful!"

"Isn't it? So you can stop worrying about money for a while can't you?"

"Well you haven't got it yet have you?"

"Don't fret gorgeous, I've got a feeling that this one's in the bag"

"As long as you're sure"

"Amy, I've never been surer of anything"

"It's about time we had a bit of luck"

"Babe, I've a feeling that our luck's about to change for ever"

Chapter 20

THE WAY I LOOK AT it, no one on the legal side of things is looking for this cash, so no one will raise an eyebrow if I deposit a few grand into the current account will they?

AMY IS OVER THE MOON and convinced that the money has come from a large bonus, so everything is peachy. I can spoil her like she deserves and she won't be worried about paying the bills. It goes without saying that we can't go buying anything large as we don't want to raise any suspicions in the private sector, if you know what I mean? But a few clothes, stuff for the kids and bits and pieces for the house will be just fine.

I'M GOING TO TAKE SATURDAY night off and take her out for a meal. Just the two of us. Her mother can baby-sit. She loves having the kids and invariably spoils them rotten. I can't wait. It's been too long since we've had a night to ourselves and although she's six months pregnant, I know she'll enjoy it too.

I'M GOING TO HAVE TO keep the rest of the money in hiding for the time being, until I work out what to do with it. Granted it's going to be very handy to just take a few quid here and there for the everyday things; big Asda shop, petrol, clothes and the like, but I can't just keep it there in the workshop until it's whittled away to nothing can I? That would definitely be a crime. No, I'm going to have to find a way of investing it so as it doesn't raise any eyebrows. Nice and subtle so even Amy doesn't know.

THAT'S WHERE IT'S HIDDEN BY the way, in a large, locked tool chest in my brick workshop at the bottom of the garden. Sounds unimaginative, I know, but I couldn't think of a better place. Amy very rarely goes in there and I always keep my toolboxes locked as a matter of course. She knows that. She'll never have a reason to go looking in there anyway, so it's fine on that score. It's not as if the law are looking for the money either, so there's no need for plod to come a calling for a nosey. I thought about other places such as the office or a mate's house, but this is by far and away the safest and most convenient. No need to get anyone else involved.

I'M THINKING PROPERTY COULD BE a winner. Some of the new apartments going up in town can be bought very reasonably off plan for a small deposit and the rental income will more than pay for the mortgage. The hard part about that will be organising an account that I can pay the deposit from. I'm sure that's sortable though.

I'VE GOT TO ADMIT, IT'S a fantastic feeling, knowing that I've got enough of the folding stuff to pay for all eventualities. The pressure is well and truly off and I can almost physically feel the weight lifted from my shoulders. This was a very good idea. This was the best decision I've made in decades. I know that the fifteen year old girl's face will flash up in my mind, probably for the rest of my days and that's just something I'm going to have to learn to live with, but, and it pains me to admit, it was still worth it. The look on Amy's face alone is worth a million heists, and a million deaths. I haven't seen her this relaxed for ages and that can only be good news for our unborn child. It's like someone has taken ten years off've her. She is positively buzzing and it thrills me no end to know that I'm the reason, that I've done something to sort out the mess we were in.

THERE IT IS AGAIN, THE girl's face. How sad am I? I don't even know her name. It was on the news enough but I didn't even take the time to listen long enough to take in her name. There was nothing I could do though was there? It was a situation beyond my control. If that steg head hadn't've got greedy and bloody stupid, the girl would still be alive. But for how long with a heroin habit?

55

Saying that, if the steg head hadn't've got so greedy and got himself shot, we wouldn't be half as minted as we are now would we? It's catch twenty-two I'm afraid. The fact remains that I had no choice. It's that simple. No choice. She was just a filthy smack head anyway. Just another junkie who would beg and steal to feed her habit. I've probably saved a few old ladies from a horrendous mugging. I've probably saved society from another financial burden, which it has no way of supporting. Filthy, fucking, baghead. That's all she was. Pimper's paradise. Funny how lyrics spring up at the most unexpected moments.

ALL THAT'S IMMATERIAL NOW ANYWAY. What's done's done. Goodnight Vienna. It's amazing how money can act as an emotional analgesic. All I have to do is think about that lovely, big stash out there in the garden and what it means to my family and all the guilt melts away. Well, almost.

Chapter 21

Saturday night and the meal is fantastic. I've taken her to Meet on Brunswick Street. It's an Argentinean Steak house of all things and it's absolutely spot on. I kind of know the owner from a door I used to work on and he's making a proper fuss of us. The steak is unbelievable and I just don't want to stop eating. Amy's lapping it up too. She loves steak, even more so now she's pregnant and you just don't get any finer.

She picks up her glass, takes a long sip of her Shloer and fixes me with her eyes.

"So what happens when this bonus runs out then?"

I'm that engrossed in my meal, it takes me a moment to register what she's asking.

"Eh?"

"This bonus, it's not going to last for ever is it? What happens when it's gone? We're back to basics again aren't we?"

"No babe, on the contrary, this is just the start. Once word gets about there'll be others coming in for the same. This is just the beginning"

"Do you think?" she asks with those huge piercing eyes burning holes through to the back of my head.

"I know babe. Don't worry. We're on the up"

"So you can stop working on the doors then?"

Bugger. I hadn't thought about this. I can't stop yet can I? Don't want to raise any suspicion so soon after the event.

"Eventually babe yeah. Got to make sure it all ticks over and wait 'til a few more bonuses start to roll in but yeah, eventually, of course. Sooner the better"

I think I'm stressing the point a bit too much here but she doesn't appear to have got on to it.

"That's when I'll relax Sammy. When you don't have to put yourself at risk anymore"

"Won't be long now kid I promise you"

Chapter 22

I'VE BEEN LOOKING INTO THIS property lark and I must say it looks promising. There's a few apartments I've got my eye on. One in particular is absolutely stunning. It's a studio on Cheapside off Dale Street and it looks like a footballer's place. Well, maybe not quite that plush but it's definitely classy. I went to see it yesterday lunch time. Massive living room with a pull down bed of all things, on the back wall. Slate floor and a sunken bath. It's up for a hundred and forty but I'm thinking I'll offer them one thirty and see how we go. A fifteen percent deposit for the buy to let mortgage will set me back just short of twenty grand but I can well afford that. The rental income will stack up to around six hundred per month so I'm quids in for the repayments. This is just far too fucking easy. The capital growth over the next ten years will be most acceptable and when I eventually come to sell it, we'll be laughing. I'm going to have to blag Amy about quite a few bonuses as the years go buy, but, judging from her recent form, she'll be fine.

Can't get my mind off that studio though. If I was a single man I'd well be living there. Right in the centre of town. I could walk to work for both jobs.

Never mind all that now though, how am I going to get an account to get this money into and pay it out of with no one being suspicious? I suppose I could just go to a different bank than our own and open a personal account. It might look a bit suss if I open it with twenty large though mightn't it? How the fuck do these big time fellas stash their cash when they've got no visible means of income? That's what I'd like to know. There must be a way. Maybe there's a certain limit that banks have before they'll inform the authorities? Maybe if you put in lower than say fifteen grand in cash they'll leave you alone? I wish there was someone I could ask who I could trust. Someone who knows the banking world inside out and knows the loopholes and pitfalls. But where will I find such a person? Maybe Terry'll have some ideas. I'll have a word on Sunday.

CHAPTER 23

It's Sunday night, I'm here at the Oak and there's no Terry. This is not good. He's not answering his phone and no one has heard from him. He hasn't rung in to say he's not working and this is making me very edgy. Terry never fails to turn in. Never. He's a reliable as a Swiss clock when it comes to work and his absence is unnerving.

The possibilities of what could have happened race through my mind and I get the urge to bolt straight from here and back home to make sure everything's ok.

I fumble my phone from my trouser pocket and press speed dial 2. After four rings Amy picks up.

"Hello?" she asks warily. I never call at this time.

"Hiya Babe, you ok?"

"I'm fine Sammy, what's up?"

"Nothing, just wanted to hear your voice"

"Why what's going on?"

"Nothing Babe honest, I'm just bored here on my Jack Jones"

"Your on your own?"

"Yeah Terry hasn't turned in"

"Is that safe?"

"Yeah, H is sending someone down now, no problems"

"Oh, good"

"The kids asleep?"

"I hope so it's half past ten"

Stupid question. If I carry on like this I *will* make her suspicious.

"Ok then sexy, I'll see you when I get in"

"Take care"

"You too. Love you"

"Love you too Sammy"

Soft I know but the tears are welling up in my eyes as I press the red button to end the call. God, I love her so much and to think that I've put her and the kids in anyway at risk gives me physical pain.

Pull yourself together Sammy lad. All that's happened is that Terry hasn't turned up for work. That's all. Plain and simple. He's probably pissed up or balls deep in some poor unfortunate starlet that he's promised the earth to. Just wish he'd answer his phone though. It 's not like it's turned off. It just rings through to the voicemail. I've left several messages but still no return call.

Answer the fuckin' phone Terry for fuck's sake! Calm down Sammy lad, he's probably left it in a taxi or something. That'll be it. He'll have gone out without it and it's sitting in his flat, chirping away to no one in particular.

I hate this because it's out of my control. All that business last week, the heists and that. It didn't exactly go according to plan I know, but at least I had control of the situation as it happened. I was there, in at ground zero, on the ball, but this? This is pure torture and all I can do is wait.

What if the Bucks have found out about our little rendezvous? What if they've already dispatched Terry and are on the way to sort my good self out?

Stop! How the fuck could they know? Eh? How the fuck could they possibly have found anything out? They don't know fuck all. They're as in the dark as the plod are. We are clear of all of it. Unmarked, unscathed without so much as a blemish. We took care of business that night in a complete and permanent way. No matter who the shitbag was related to, he wasn't going to go telling anyone that he's bumping his own dealers was he? No chance. His own family would fill him in for that no two ways about it. It's something you just don't do.

There will be a perfectly reasonable explanation for Terry's absence and as soon as find out what it is I'll be a happy man.

CHAPTER 24

IT'S NOW MONDAY AFTERNOON AND I've just had that all important call from Terry. It transpires that the little twat was indeed balls deep and had left his phone on silent so as not to be disturbed.

What a wanker? Here's me having kittens and he's sunk to the nuts. Says he lost track of time and by the time he realised, it was too late to ring in. Must have been some judy to make him forget he had to go to work. My blood pressure has dropped considerably since receiving this news, needless to say, and in hindsight it's quite laughable. Put the fear of god into me at the time though I don't mind saying. Anyway, all's well that ends well eh? I just hope this has ended. Terry says he's got a proposition for me to be discussed next Sunday and I'm wondering what it can be. If it's anything on the shady side he can forget it. My days of risky enterprise are well and truly over. Goodnight Vienna.

CHAPTER 25

I'VE TOOK THE PLUNGE AND been to the bank. I've been to a few banks as it happens, three in total and deposited ten grand in each brand new account and do you know what? The nice people who opened the accounts for me didn't even flinch when I handed over my grubby little bundles of used notes. Not a flicker. No questions, no suspicious looks, just a warm smile and friendly handshake before I left. Fantastic! Absolutely made up. Should have done this last week. I now have money residing in three major high street banks, not including our own bank, which I naturally gave a miss.

Maybe I could have put more away. Maybe I should have gone for twenty in each. Don't want to be too greedy though do I? Don't want to get careless. Once the money has gone out of these accounts for the deposits on the flats I'm buying, I'll put a little more in. Just a dribble though. Keep my head down under the radar so to speak. Always err on the side of caution. Never get too cocky. Don't want to spoil a good thing.

I can keep all the details in the spare filing cabinet at the office under lock and key. I've asked for all mail to be sent there as well, so it should all tie in nicely.

There's a spring in my step as I bounce along Victoria Street and past Vida's. What a shitty looking dive it is in the daylight. Squalid and cheap. Won't be long now though. Won't be long at all til' I can swerve it for good. I can't take the smile from my face and I'm drawing some inquisitive looks from passers by. Couldn't give a toss though. Couldn't care one bit. Let them look. Let them see the face of a man who is pulling himself out of mediocrity and into the good life for the benefit of his loving family. I am on top of the world. King of creation. Lord of all I survey. Well, not quite.

CHAPTER 26

SO IT'S SUNDAY NIGHT AGAIN and we're here at the Oak. After half an hour of the usual banter I'm eager to know about this proposition.

"Well la, the thing is" Terry starts as the grin cracks his face in two "We've got a certain amount of disposable income at the minute haven't we?"

"And..?"

"And, money makes money right?"

"And..?"

"And, there's a certain fella I know wants to get rid of eight keys of not so high grade bugle for the knockdown price of fifteens"

"And..?"

"And la, we can move it on to aul' Rodders up there in the Himalayas for twenty fives the same day. That's another forty grand profit each for one day's graft"

"What if he tests it again?" is the first question that springs to mind.

"He won't. He'll take my word that it's from the same batch as the others"

"And what about when his customers start to complain?"

"We'll be long gone by then won't we? Done and dusted. Out of the industry for good"

"But what if he comes looking for us?" I enquire "He's only in Keswick"

"Rodney? Do me a favour. He may have it to himself up there in hick town but he's a fish out of water down here. Besides, the yokels round them parts won't have a clue anyway will they? Half of them'd snort fuckin' VIM if they thought it'd give them a buzz wouldn't they?"

"I suppose so" I answer, still not entirely convinced.

"So what d'you reckon then?"

I must admit it is very tempting, very tempting indeed. I really can't believe there's this much money to be made in such a short space of time for so little effort. Surely there must be a catch. Surely to god somebody somewhere will put a stop to this madness. How can we be allowed to make this sort of dough? Mad as it seems, we are doing. But when do I stop? I told myself after the last trip to Keswick that it would be the end of my criminal career. I told myself I'd be happy with what I'd already got, but, in the end I was telling myself lies. Oh well, in for a penny...

"Fuck it, why not?"

"That's the spirit!" Terry gleefully chirps as he hops from one foot to the other in sheer joy "You know it makes sense" he adds in his best Del Boy accent.

CHAPTER 27

AND SO THE ROLLER COASTER rides on, gathering momentum like an arrow from a bow. And it would seem that I'm happy with it…so far. Try as I might I can't think of a reason not to go with the flow. After all, I've already crossed over the line between law abiding citizen and common criminal so I might as well make hay while the sun shines mightn't I? No reason to look a gift horse in the mouth. Another forty grand would go down very nicely and would look just charming stashed away in my workshop.

I've had my eye on a new car too. Nothing too ostentatious, just a nice newer Golf or Beemer or something. The old Golf is still a nice motor but it's starting to look a little dated if you catch my drift. Just that little bit too retro and it's starting to sound a bit clunky here and there. There's a few whines and whistles that seem to be getting louder. The old workhorse needs putting out to graze.

I could tell Amy the new car's a company car, especially if it's a saloon. A three series or an A4. That would be entirely believable wouldn't it? Very feasible. Nothing out of the ordinary there. Here I go again, more lies. More duplicity. It's amazing how one lie leads to another isn't it? How far will I have to go though? How many lies will I have to tell until all this is behind us and we're on an even keel? Somebody once told me that the art to being a good liar is having an excellent memory. Well that's me fucked for a start isn't it? I have a head like a sieve as Amy delights in reminding me. My short term memory is awful at best so I'm going to have to make a concerted effort to put all the lies in order in my head. Possibly even write them down. Amy's always on at me to make lists. Could be incriminating evidence if found though couldn't it? Could be very risky. We'll have to see.

We gave the shooter back to Jerry Jacobs by the way. He didn't bat an eyelid either. Just like handing back a rented film at the DVD shop. So casual, so nonchalant, as if handling an illegal, deadly weapon is the most natural thing in the world. He was obviously oblivious to the fact that there was a rogue bullet in the chamber. There's no need for him to know that little pearl of wisdom. The big juicehead just grinned and offered us a brew. His gaff is something else by the way. Two semis knocked into one with a massive extension on the back. The interior looks like something out of Grand Designs. Absolutely spotless. State of the art fucking everything and I do mean everything. And there's him slouched in the middle of it all in an old Lacoste trackie scratching his knackers while his peroxide blonde girlfriend cleans around him like an obsessive.

Terry exchanged a bit of banter with him for a while but I really couldn't be bothered conversing with him any more than was necessary to be perfectly honest. He's one of them JJ, bit of a dinosaur in today's world know what I mean? Thinks he can live forever on his reputation. Thinks that just because he had a fight or two fifteen or twenty years ago that he's untouchable now. But times have changed Jerry lad. There's little rats out there who'll shoot you just to see what it feels like. Just to have that accolade that they've plugged somebody, especially someone like you. That would have definite kudos in the shitty little world in which they live. All these little shitbags who have watched one too many gangster films or heard one too many stories about the big fellas with the big money and they can't see why they shouldn't have some of it. I fucking hate them and their shitty little attitudes. All screwed up faces and scowls. Swaggering along in the obligatory trackie bottoms and hoodies, every one of them no more than nine stone dripping wet. Not a decent punch in any of them. Fucking scum. There's no way on this earth that my kids are going to turn out like that. Not a chance. First sign of any of that, hanging around with the wrong crowd and all that and I'll have to intervene for the good of my kids. Even if it means going out and bladdering the lot of their new mates I'll do it. It simply will not be allowed to happen.

After we left JJ's Terry said something that made me stop and think. Just as we were leaving Old Swan he casually let slip that his cousin would be more than willing to take the new gear up to Keswick for us. What the fuck is he doing telling his cousin about all of this? What the fuck is he doing telling anyone anything about this? I put this to him in a concerned manner and his response alarmed me.

"Don't worry la, he's sound is our Finchy, all day la, no worries" he replied completely oblivious to my immediate concern.

"That's as maybe Terry but I thought we agreed to keep this between ourselves? You haven't told him the whole story have you?"

"Of course I haven't, fuckin' hell la d'you think I'm that stupid? No, I just told him that we had to move a bit of the other and I knew he'd be up for it. He already thinks I'm a bit shifty just cos' of the fact that I work on the doors and that doesn't he? But he's sound mate, a hundred and ten percent all day, no questions asked"

"No la, I'm sorry but I'm not happy with it at all. This needs to be kept in house" I told him "No outsiders, not even family. We'll take the gear ourselves, just like last time. We need to be in at ground zero, know what I mean? We can't leave this to anyone not considerin' that it's substandard gear"

"Alright la but he's not gonna be happy" Terry replied pouring petrol on the flames of my anger.

"I really couldn't give a shit to be perfectly honest kidder. The emotional well being of your family doesn't rate high on my list of priorities next to my liberty and safety, get me?" Maybe a little harsh but I'm having trouble understanding the lad's logic.

"Alright la, fair enough" he replied a little testily "It was just an idea"

"Yeah well let's just forget about eh?"

"If you say so"

It still bothers me though. The fact that he was so willing to involve someone else in this little quagmire alarms me greatly. It all just adds weight to the argument that the only way to keep something to yourself is to be the only one involved. The only one with overall knowledge. Maybe I should have left Terry in that house with the steg head and the junkie. That would've well and truly tied up all loose ends wouldn't it? That would've made me a lot safer with everything under my control and no extraneous variables.

What the fuck am I on about now? Will you have a listen to Tony Montana here. What a fuckin' whopper? Like I'm going to slot Terry. Fucking mouth that he is, I'm not about to murder the dopey cunt am I?

I do get ahead of myself sometimes don't I? Terry's just going to have to pull the reigns in a bit, that's all. Just slow down and think a little. I suppose he's only in his twenties and still a bit raw. Still raring to go. Still juiced up on his own natural testosterone and adrenalin. I'm just going to have to guide the lad aren't I? Be a kind of life mentor if you will. But I'm not going to kill him am I? Don't be fucking daft.

Chapter 28

CHAOS REIGNS IN OUR HOUSE this morning. Absolute chaos. My beautiful daughter came downstairs to find her beloved cat dead in his basket. I'm amazed he lasted this long to be perfectly honest. Battled to the end he did.

She is absolutely distraught though, poor kid and it breaks my heart to see her so upset. She is absolutely inconsolable and I'm beginning to get a little worried about her. She just won't stop crying. She's been going for two hours now and she's starting to shiver. Amy has called the doctor out to be on the safe side and he'd better hurry up. I feel completely helpless. I've tried to comfort her, to put my arms around her and hold her safe but it doesn't seem to make a difference. If anyone can calm her down it's me. She's always been a Daddy's girl, right from early on. It's always been me she's come running to in the past when she's upset or hurt herself and she's always calmed when she's in my arms. Not today though. I have to admit, the tears are welling up in my own eyes. I can't stand to see her like this and there's nothing I can do. Nothing I can say.

The little fella's upset as well, but I don't think he's quite grasped the situation like she has. I think he's more upset because everybody else is, rather than for the loss of our family pet.

We all sit huddled on the couch, united in our grief. Nobody is going to school or work today. Today we need to stay together as a family, for the sake of Molly's sanity if nothing else.

I need to calm Amy down and stop her worrying about Molly. Stress on the unborn baby can be extremely dangerous at this stage so I need to distract her.

"Connor, I need you to be a big boy for me now, can you do that?" I ask of my son.

"Ok Dad!" he chirps up, sorrow briefly forgotten in the wake of a potential position of responsibility.

"I need you to go upstairs with Mummy and look after her while she gets dressed, can you do that for me?"

"No problem Dad" he says "Just you leave it to me"

Bless his cotton socks he's a little belter.

"That's my boy," I tell him as I wink at Amy and motion for her to go upstairs.

"Come on Mum" He tells her in a manner far beyond his years as he leads her by the hand "Let's get you dressed"

The smile between Amy and myself breaks the tension and she lets herself be led away by this overenthusiastic little powerhouse.

As they leave the room I turn to Molly. Her sobbing has subsided a little now and her eyes have a far away look as she whimpers and shivers and stares off into the middle distance.

"Molly I need you to listen to me now, can you do that for Daddy?"

There's a brief flicker of recognition and I take my opportunity while it's there.

"I know you're very upset about Paisley sweetheart, we all are. And I know you think the world is ending and that this is the worse day of your life and it probably is so far, but I need you to be a big strong girl for me now, ok? I need you to try and listen to Daddy because I need you to help me for Mummy's sake, can you do that?"

Her eyes suddenly focus and she fixes me with a piercing stare.

"Why, what's wrong with Mummy?" she demands of me, back in the land of the living in an instant, concern streaking across her dainty little face.

"Nothing's wrong with Mummy sweetheart" I tell her trying to keep my voice on an even keel, calm and gentle "She's fine, she's just very worried about you munchkin, we all are"

"I'm fine" she lies wiping the tears from her face.

"No you're not, you're very, very upset and you've got every right to be. You loved Paisley and it's very difficult when someone you love dies. It feels like your whole world's been ripped apart and it breaks your heart"

She starts to cry again but this time she buries her head deep into my chest, throws her arms around me and really lets rip.

"That's right sweetheart, you let it all out on Daddy" I tell her as I stroke her hair and hold her as close to me as possible "Daddy's here…Daddy's here"

After a couple of minutes she gains control again and looks me square in the face.

"It's not fair though Daddy, why did Paisley have to die?"

"He was very old babe wasn't he? He'd had a good, happy, long life and you made it extra special. He won't be in any pain now will he? He'll be at peace"

"He won't though will he?" she replies sharply "Cos' there's no cat heaven!"

D'you know if that Miss Turnbull was a man I'd go into that school and knock her out the miserable bitch.

"What has Daddy told you about what Miss Turnbull said, eh? Don't you listen to a word she says about this d'you here me? She may be a good teacher but she's a little confused when it comes to the afterlife"

"She says that a good Christian doesn't believe that animals have souls and that the idea of a cat heaven is preposetrows or something"

"Preposterous sweetheart, I think she meant preposterous" Miss Turnbull has just earned herself a little visit from yours truly. This is far beyond the call of duty of a teacher.

"Miss Turnbull grew up a long time ago when we didn't know what we know now and sometimes people get silly ideas about a lot of things. Who're you going to believe though eh? Miss Turnbull or Daddy?"

"I believe you Daddy but why would she say that?"

Very good question, very good question indeed. It's all well and good having religious beliefs but forcing them on a child like this is unforgivable.

"Like I say sweetheart, she's just a bit confused, that's all. Paisley will be up there now chasing mice and eating steak you mark my words"

"Do you really think so?" She asks with huge red eyes filled with hope.

"I know so"

CHAPTER 29

So we're at the lad's house who's going to sell us the gear and I'm instantly not happy.

He is a rat. No two ways about it, he is a bonifide, hundred percent, rat. Nineteen years old if he's a day. Hoodie, trackies, scowl, at rat.

Attitude on the prick as well. Thinks he's the boy this lad. Thinks he's lord of all he surveys. Arrogant cunt. Horrible, arrogant cunt. I want to grab him by the neck and choke the life out of him. I want to kick him until he bleeds. I want to obliterate him. I want to end his life.

When Terry introduced us he gave me a look as if to say 'Yeah, and who the fuck are you?' and continued talking to Terry. Cheeky twat. He's going to get it this one. Maybe not today but in the not too distant future, he's going to have his comeuppance. I'll see to that personally. Your card is well and truly marked lad. End of story.

The gear is sitting on the kitchen table in kilo bundles and Terry hastily packs them into the sports bag, then hands the prick the money.

"I won't bother counting it" he informs us "You know if it's not all there I'll come lookin' you"

Very nearly. Very fucking nearly bit his screwed up little face off.

"And what d'you mean by that?" I enquire, my voice barely masking my rage.

"Eh?" he replies sullenly.

"You sayin' we're gonna rip you off here or what?"

"You wanna teach him a few manners Terry lad" he says to my partner in crime with a look of annoyance on his twisted little dial.

That's the one. Before I'm even aware of what I'm doing, I've grabbed him by the throat and he's up against the wall. I can feel the cartilage of his windpipe as my fingers close around it. He's desperately trying to breath. Gasping, choking, suffocating.

Terry's on my back trying to pull me away but the adrenalin coursing through my veins is giving me superhuman strength and I brush him away with my spare hand.

I look deep into my victim's ever reddening eyes as my grip tightens. He is terrified now. Absolutely petrified. He thinks he's going to die. He may well yet, I haven't decided. Haven't made my mind up whether I'm going to let this scum carry on breathing or not. It would make sense to kill him to be perfectly honest. Just end his life here, take the gear and keep the money. I wouldn't lose any sleep over this wretch. No way. Wouldn't bat an eyelid. Who would know? Terry would. Can he keep a secret? Questionable at the moment. Would he tell? Who knows? Can he be trusted? That's to be seen.

The lad's lips are going blue now and he's starting to struggle less. Going limp. Giving up. Accepting his fate. Don't think I'll kill him today though. Think I'll let him live. Let him see the error of his ways and apologise when he's able to.

I release my grip and he falls to the floor, still gasping for breath. I thought he would be able to breath when I let him go but he's still convulsing, struggling to draw breath and then I see it. Looking at his throat I can see that I've crushed and twisted his windpipe. I kneel down and try to manipulate it so as he can breath but it's no good and in a matter on seconds his life slips away.

I look around at Terry and he's eyeing me with nothing short of revulsion.

"What?" I ask him as he looks from my face to the body on the floor.

"What the fuck are you doing?" He asks incredulously, face frozen in a rictus of horror.

"Fuckin' asked for it didn't he?"

"You fuckin' what?" Terry spits "He asked for it? All's he did was give a bit of cheek and you've slotted him"

"Look, I didn't mean to kill the lad alright? Just meant to scare him a bit, that's all"

"Well you've done more than scare him haven't you? Fuckin' hell la we're turning into fuckin' serial killers here"

"Are we fuck" I blast him, bringing him back to reality "No one's gonna miss the little cunt, end of the day, are they, so we're quids in aren't we?"

"How d'you mean" Terry asks blankly.

"Well we don't have to pay him for the gear now do we?"

Terry shakes his head in disbelief "What are you gonna do? Knock off every dealer in Liverpool so's you don't have to pay them?"

"Don't talk daft. Let's just get the gear and the dough and get the fuck out of here. We can discuss this later"

But Terry's eyeing me very cautiously now. He's looking me over like I'm a ticking bomb waiting to go off at any minute. And maybe he's right.

CHAPTER 30

"MR JACKSON, HOW CAN I help you?" Miss Turnbull asks me as she approaches, hand outstretched, plastic smile underpinning her ageing face.

I refrain from shaking her hand and it remains floating in mid air, waiting for it's opposite number to make the greeting complete.

"I need to talk to you about Molly" I tell her in as level a tone as I can manage.

The hand gets the message and hesitantly returns to it's owners side.

"Certainly" she replies and leads the way to her office "Please have a seat" she adds as she gestures towards an old leather armchair. I sink into it and at once I'm at a disadvantage. I'm almost lying down, so low is the chair that even when I sit forward, I feel like a little boy looking up at the teacher. Good move Miss Turnbull, very good move.

"Now, what seems to be the problem?" she asks as she glowers down at me.

"Well miss Turnbull, as you're aware, our cat has recently passed away and I'm sure you haven't failed to notice that Molly has taken it quite badly"

"Yes the poor thing, she does seem quite upset" she offers with artificial sympathy.

"And things have been made worse for her by your flippancy over the possibility of the cat having an afterlife" Now I feel stupid. I feel absolutely fucking ridiculous if I'm honest. I hadn't quite thought about how I was going to put this and it's not coming out very well. Oh well. I press on for Molly.

"Surely you're not suggesting that you encourage this pagan idea of animals having souls are you Mr Jackson" Thank you miss Turnbull, you've just moved me up a notch.

"What I encourage my daughter to believe is entirely my choice"

"But Mr Jackson" she persists "Surely the teachings of the Christian faith tell us that this is not so. The idea that animals have souls is preposterous" There it is. Molly nearly got it right.

"Correct me if I'm wrong Miss Turnbull but this is a non-denominational school"

"Well yes but..."

"Well there you have it. I'll thank you not to go ramming your religious beliefs down my daughters throat, especially when she is in such an emotional state"

"Mr Jackson, I hardly think...,"

"Frankly Miss Turnbull, I don't really care what you think, just leave my daughter to grieve in her own way"

And with that, I lift myself from the floor level armchair with as much dignity as is possible and march from the room.

CHAPTER 31

LOOKING BACK AT THE OTHER night I don't know what came over me. The lad was an insolent little prick but did he deserve to die? Probably not, no.

Terry's naturally concerned and who can blame him? This is the third person to die in the name of our quest for riches and glory and it's not sitting very well with him. I don't know why he's worrying though. There's no possible way we can be linked with this one either. As is becoming the norm, we covered our tracks, or rather I covered our tracks.

The gas trick worked a treat again, only this time I put a can of beans in the microwave. It still had the same effect. The house went up like a roman candle. All evidence destroyed. All trace wiped away. A clean slate again.

But Terry's still worried. I can see it in his face and hear in his voice. He's a very troubled man at the minute and it's up to me to reassure him, to nurture him. He'll be fine once we've got the money for this new batch of gear, I'm sure of it. Does like his cash does our Terrance. Oh yes. That's a definite. His eyes light up like Bunsen burners in the presence of used banknotes. It's like a reaction. If you watch him closely you can see his breathing speed up and you can almost see the veins pulsing in his neck. It's a fatal flaw if you will.

We're going to see Rodney tomorrow and there's another hundred grand each. Fucking marvellous. Tremendous. Outstanding. Think I'm going to have to get a bigger tool chest. Too easy. Really, too easy.

Three deaths is a lot though. More than a lot, it's too much. None of them were intentional though were they? It's not as if we set out to do them in is it? Just an unfortunate set of circumstances, that's all. Just plain unlucky and I do feel for them, for their families. Even though two of them were out and out no marks, they still must've had families who cared for them mustn't they? And it's them that I feel for.

These deaths, however, are not the first I have on my conscience. Oh no. That takes me way back. All the way back to the early eighties, to little Jimmy Campbell. Poor little fucker. He never wanted to try the lighter gas we were sniffing. Always refused, even though we gave him so much stick, he always stuck to his guns. And we did give him hell. Time and time again we tried every trick in the book to get him to have a go but he was adamant. He'd just sit and watch as me and Adam Fletcher got absolutely off our barnetts, giggling like idiots. He'd just sit and watch and shake his head.

Then one day he capitulated for some reason I can't quite fathom, and took the can in his hand. One sniff later he began to convulse and fell to the ground fitting like an epileptic.

We thought he was messing about at first and the pair of us rolled about laughing at him. It soon became evident though, that all wasn't well and panic set in.

We did try to help him, we honestly did, but we didn't have a clue. First aid was a mystery to us, panic eventually won and we fled, leaving our friend shuddering and shaking with his eyes rolled back in his head.

It was the Monday morning in school that we found out that he had died.

We were sat in our form and his chair was empty. We just assumed that he was having the day off sick, but when the teacher came in, we knew from his face that it was serious.

"Listen up" the teacher said, his voice trembling with the effort of keeping his composure "Everybody take your seats and stop talking I have something I need to tell you"

An eerie hush fell across the class as everyone clocked the grave expression of our form teacher. He took a few moments to compose himself the put his best foot forward.

"Unfortunately" he began, his adam's apple bobbing up and down like a yoyo "One of our students... James Campbell, won't be coming into school today... In fact he won't be coming in again" The strain clearly visible on his face now as he tried to bring himself to the point where he could tell us the full, grisly facts.

"There has been an unfortunate accident" there it was again, that word, unfortunate "and James has died"

An audible shockwave rippled through the class. Girls began to cry and lads began to cough. I just glowered at Adam across the classroom, my eyes telling him 'Do not say a word' in no uncertain terms.

The feeling of self revulsion almost made me vomit as I struggled to come to terms with what had happened. We had left him to die. We had badgered him, *forced* him to join in our little game and it had cost him his life.

I didn't have a proper night's sleep for weeks and I lost a stone in weight, which I could ill afford to lose. In the end my mum took me to the doctors she was so worried.

My school work fell by the wayside and my zest for life dwindled.

It took me a long time to get over it but poor Adam never did. One year after, on the anniversary of Jimmy's death, he took his own life. His parents came home from work to find him hanging from a rope tied through the loft hatch to the rafters. A sort of makeshift gallows if you will.

In his suicide note he told of his guilt at making Jimmy take the lighter gas and leaving him to die, but he never mentioned my name. I could've kissed him for that. There was the odd one or two gossips who had their suspicions though, but nobody dared say anything to me by that stage. Word had spread that I was unstable, unpredictable and very possibly dangerous, so I was given a wide berth by all but Amy. She was the only one who offered my any form of empathy or even sympathy and she is the only person to this day that I have ever told the truth to. She was amazingly understanding as well, considering that I had told her I was an accessory in the death of one of our classmates. She didn't judge me, hate me or even blame me, she just listened to me pour my heart out time and time again, night after night after school. She was unbelievable and I fell so deeply in love with her that I couldn't imagine my life without her. I still can't. I know it's a cliché, but she is my soul mate. No two ways about it, she is the other half of me and to imagine a world without her is to take a trip to hell. We've been together now for twenty years. We've travelled the globe together, we've grown together and we'll be together until we die. This I am sure of. There is no doubt in my mind that we will be together through to our autumn years. Two old codgers like Paul Simon's bookends. United in our mutual devotion. I'm running away with myself here, I know, but I can't help the way that I feel. She is my rock and without her I am nothing.

That's what troubles me most about this sordid little world into which I find myself falling with apparent ease. This is a risk to our relationship. Even though I've done it all for her and the kids, I doubt she would see it that way and if she were to find out about any of this, well, the consequences don't even bare thinking about.

Chapter 32

Rodney is the same as last time, pleasant enough, but eager to get down to business.

There's a moment where he looks like he wants to test the gear, but Terry's patter soon reassures him and he dishes out the dosh with his usual nonchalance.

Two hundred thousand pounds. I just like saying it out loud. Two hundred thousand pounds. It's wonderful to have those words pass your lips when it's in relation to your own pocket. Even split two ways, it's a magnificent sum. There's definitely a new car winging it's way to the Jackson household. Of this there is no doubt. Nice beamer or a Merc. Something a bit tasty.

Terry tries to include me in the conversation, but I'm miles away, floating on the clouds of opulence, gliding down the avenues of affluence, sailing on the sea of prosperity.

"Isn't that right Sam?"

"What's that?" I reply, dragging myself from my reverie.

"We're having an early retirement from the narcotics industry aren't we?"

"Oh, yeah, right" I reply sounding like I've been getting high on our own supply.

"Without a doubt" Terry continues "This is the last consignment that we'll be bringing"

"That's a real shame that is Tirroye, real shame. This gear's gone down very well in local circles loike"

"Such is life Rodders me old mucker"

"Well, you know where I am if yow come across any more of the same. Just give old Rodney a bell and oil 'ave the readies waitin' for yow"

Very nice to know that Rodney, very nice.

CHAPTER 33

THE MONEY ONLY JUST FITS into my tool chest and I have to literally jump on the lid to get it closed. This is a nice predicament to have. To have that much cash that I have to batter it down to close the lid. It's an annoyance that I really don't mind to be fair.

I bought a mitre saw from B+Q, took it out of the box and left it in the office, then filled the empty box with the cash to take it home. Amy never suspected a thing when I carried it straight out to the workshop. A very cunning plan even if I do say so myself. More deception though. More lies and this worries me. I'm becoming very proficient in my duplicity. It's becoming second nature to me so easily.

Terry's coming into the office today for a 'chat'. Wonder what that's all about? He sounded ok on the phone so it must be something other than what's been going on lately.

It's been a week now since the last job and although the lad's death has been all over the news, there has been no interest in our good selves. No one would ever think of linking us with all of that, neither the bizzies nor the private sector. We are home and hosed. Free as a bird. Clean as a whistle.

There's only one weak link in the chain and that's Terry. I think he's calmed down enough now though. He's had a week to come to terms with all that's gone on and I think he's seeing things from a more practical point of view now. If we both sit tight and stay tight lipped then we'll sail through this. Nobody but nobody would ever suspect Terry and myself, I'm one hundred percent sure of the fact. The little rat from last week, it turns out, was a bag man for Jerry Jacobs. Small fucking world isn't it? Old JJ's on the rampage by all accounts, he's fuming. Turning everybody over to try and find the culprit. The rat mustn't have told him that he was doing business with Terry and myself or we'd know about it by now in no uncertain terms. So it's happy days. Just hope Terry can see it that way. He'll come round, I'm sure of it. Once we've discussed it and put all the cards on the table he'll be fine.

I've bought the apartment I was after by the way. We complete in a couple of weeks and I'm absolutely made up. I've already got a tenant waiting to move in so it's all stitched up. That was too easy as well. It was only advertised to let for three days and it was snapped up by a doctor who works at the Royal. Nice fella.

I've got my eye on another apartment up by the Carling Academy. The footings have only just gone in but the prices are very reasonable off plan. I've had a word with the developer and he seems to know what he's on about so I've reserved one. Be rude not to really wouldn't it? This has meant depositing a few more notes in each of the bank accounts but as with last time, no one so much as raised an eyebrow. Too easy.

I got the new motor as well. Nice two year old BMW 323. Jet black, tinted windows, huge alloys. Very me. Amy thinks it's a company car and she's having the old Golf as a run around.

Everything's slotting into place. Things are calming down and life seems to be getting back on an even keel again. Hopefully I can start to put all the nastiness behind me now and get on with enjoying the spoils. But that ultimately rests with Terry though doesn't it?

CHAPTER 34

THE BUZZER INDICATES THAT SOMEONE wishes to gain entrance to the building and I pick up the intercom phone to see who it is.

"Hello LIFT, can I help you?"

"Alright la it's me" Terry's dulcet tones float through the earpiece.

I push the button to open the door and await his arrival.

Minutes later he's in the office and sat down in the chair opposite.

"Well?" I ask "What's goin' on?"

"Shit has well and truly hit the fan la"

My stomach shifts in an uneasy manner. This does not sound good.

"How d'you mean?" I enquire with a certain amount of trepidation.

"Jerry Jacobs has been nicked. They've caught him with quite a few keys of white and a couple of brown"

"Shame" I reply "Poor fella"

"That's not the worst of it la. They've only found that shooter we had 'aven't they? It was in his ken when they raided it and they've now matched it with the bullet that killed Jamie Buck so they're charging him with the murder as well"

"And how is that bad news for us? Surely that's better for us isn't it?"

"Are you for fuckin' real? He's gonna be sendin' all kinds of fellas lookin for us now isn't he?"

My heart drops to my stomach as the fabric of our comfortable little world gives way underneath me.

"Why?" I ask vacantly

"He now knows that it was us that shot Jamie Buck and I'll bet the Buck's will be on to the fact too"

This is not good. This is not good at all.

"Why the fuck didn't you tell me this pearl of wisdom this morning when you found out?" I enquire somewhat vexed by his lack of communication.

"What? Speak on the phone? Don't be fuckin' daft"

"Who the fuck is gonna be listening to us?"

"You'd be surprised la. The Bucks 'ave got a lot of fingers in a lot of pies and that includes the plod"

"For fuck's sake!" This is spiralling out of control and panic is slowly taking over my senses. My power of logical reason is dwindling and it's all I can do to think straight.

"I've left the flat" Terry continues "Packed as much as I could and left it as is"

"How would they know where we live?" The question fills me with dread.

"Big H is related to the bucks isn't he and he's got all our details"

For fuck's sake is there no one in the Liverpool underworld that isn't related?

Then the obvious hits me. Amy and the kids. I snatch my phone off the desk and frantically push speed dial two. After what seems like a lifetime it actually connects but the phone just rings out.

That's it. In a blind panic I race from the office and down the stairs to the front door. Terry is close behind me as we burst out onto the street.

"I'll come with you la, just in case" he offers as we both jump into the BM.

Scotland road is a mess of wagons and taxis and all manner of unconcerned, hapless drivers and it's all I can do to stop myself spontaneously combusting with the shear frustration of it all.

If we get there in one piece it will be a miracle.

CHAPTER 35

As we approach the house nothing looks out of place. The car screeches to a halt and I'm out of the door and across the front garden in an instant.

It takes a couple of seconds to get the key in the door, such is the tremor in my hands, but when I eventually do I'm through and into the hall.

"Amy!" I call out, panic running thick through my voice, but no answer.

I'm into every room at lightening speed but there's no sign of anyone. It takes a while for it to sink in but each room looks unusually sterile. This plays at the back of my mind as my main concern for finding Amy and the kids fills my immediate thoughts.

The last room I enter is our bedroom. Nothing. Not a sign of life. My imagination goes into overdrive. What the fuck has happened to them? Where the fuck are they? Think Sammy lad, think. Right. Molly's going to be in school isn't she? Of course she is. It's a school day after all.

Terry's looking up at me from the hall as I descend the stairs deep in thought.

"What's the score then?" he enquires.

"Haven't got a fuckin' clue" I tell him shaking my head "Not a clue"

I didn't realise on the way in but I now see, through the kitchen window, that the Golf isn't on the path. Where the hell is she?

I try her mobile again, but as before, it just rings and rings. I'm starting to feel sick with worry now, physically sick and it's a struggle to keep my lunch in it's rightful place.

What the fuck have I done? How could I have been so reckless? Remorse fills me and penetrates every cell of my body. All the money in the world isn't worth this. The fact that now, at this moment in time, my family could be in grave danger all because of a choice I've made. All because of a simple decision, lightly made on the door of the Oak one Sunday night. FUCKING PRICK! Useless fucking PRICK! What have I done? Jesus Christ please let them be safe. I'll give anything in this world or the next for them to be safe and unharmed. Why did I put them in danger like this? Why did I taint our lives with all this filthy, dirty business? Why couldn't I have refused? Said thanks but no thanks Terry lad, not for me I'm afraid, family man and all that.

The urge to turn around and knock the living shite out of Terry is almost overwhelming but it's not his fault is it? Of course it isn't. I made the decision as a responsible adult and I must be held accountable for my own actions mustn't I?

Fuck, fuck, fuck, fuck, fuck, I'm panicking now. I'm really losing control and my mind is swimming with all the horrific possibilities that could actually be happening right now. Amy's eight months pregnant. Eight months! What the fuck am I doing putting her and our unborn child at risk? I am scum. That's all there is to it, I'm scum. Worse than scum I'm worthless. I don't deserve them all.

My shoulders are starting to shake now and Terry is starting to worry.

"You alright la?" he asks with obvious concern.

I just hold my hand up to indicate that I'll be fine in a minute. That's all I can do, hold my hand up. I have lost the power of speech. My mouth is as dry as a blast furnace and twice as hot. My vision is starting to waver. My balance is leaving me. The pain in my stomach is crippling. I put out a hand to steady myself but it fails to find purchase and floats around in mid air before Terry catches hold of it and guides me to the kitchen table and sits me down on one of the chairs.

"Steady there la, steady" he tells me, but I'm not listening. I just place my head in my hands and bury my palms into the sockets of my eyes.

Silence reigns for an immeasurable amount of time until it is broken by the shrill of my mobile phone.

In a millisecond I sweep it up off the side and push the green button.

"Hello?" I enquire desperately.

"Sammy?" Amy's voice trickles down the phone, filled with concern at the obvious panic in mine.

"Amy?" please god let her be ok.

"Yes it's me. Sammy is everything alright?" Now she's worried. Think quick lad.

"I'm fine Amy, how're you?" Please, please, please!

"I fine"

"Where are you?"

"I'm at the supermarket, where're you?"

"I'm at home"

"Why?" good question.

"Just fancied the afternoon off. Thought we might spend it together"

"Well you can just go out again until later can't you?" she tells me. Then the penny drops. The house is spotless. The dining room table is set complete with candelabra and flowers. There's no sign of the kids toys anywhere.

"Aaaahh"

"Yes aaaahh" she replies "don't you show your face until at least six o'clock. The kids are staying at my mothers"

My body has now relaxed so much that my legs very nearly give way. If there is a god, thank you, thank you so much.

CHAPTER 36

THE RELIEF I FEEL IS short lived. As I drive Terry back into town the realisation hits me that this is far from over.

"What's the plan now then?" I ask him.

"How d'you mean?" he replies blankly.

"What are we gonna do about all this shit?"

"I don't know about you la but I'm getting the fuck out of here"

"What?" I ask him incredulously.

"I'm fucking off la. We're sittin' ducks round here and it's only a matter of time"

"Until what?" I ask but I already know the answer.

"You know very well what" he replies.

"JJ might not have put us together with all of that though mightn't he? After all, I bet we weren't the only ones to borrow that shooter were we?"

"And you want to hang around until he works it out do you?" Good point Terry lad. Good point. Think I'm going to have to make a few contingency plans of my own. Short-term protection until we find out the true extent of the situation. I think a holiday is called for. A couple of weeks somewhere picturesque and not far away in this country. That can be sorted this afternoon.

"Who've you got who can keep his ear to the ground?" I ask of Terry.

"Our Finchy'll keep me posted la, no problems there"

"And you'll be keeping your mobile on then?"

"Oh aye"

"That's sorted then" For the meantime.

CHAPTER 37

I ARRIVE HOME AT SIX o'clock on the dot and she's waiting for me, looking absolutely sensational. She's greets me at the door with a smile and a Jameson's and leads me inside by the hand. The smell that greets me is pure, unadulterated heaven. There are no other words to describe the aroma that hits my nostrils as I sit at the table and await the gastronomic delight. I have never tasted Chinese food like she makes in my life. She is absolutely amazing at it. She makes it all from scratch from the best ingredients. That's where she was today when she phoned, at the Chinese supermarket underneath the Tai Pan on Great Howard Street.

"Not that I'm complaining, but what have I done to deserve this?" I ask her as she floats back into the room carrying two bowls of hot and sour soup.

"What have you done? You've given us all a better life and sorted out our financial disaster that's what you've done. I'm so proud of how hard you've worked for us Sammy" she says as she kisses me on the forehead and sits down opposite me. She stares straight into my eyes with a look that says a thousand words and the pangs of guilt course through my mind like lightning. How could I lie to this wonderful human being? How could I put her in so much danger? I am most definitely not worthy of her love or her affection or her time. I'm not fit to clean her shoes.

She sees something in my eyes and a look of concern crosses her face.

"What's up Sam? You sounded really weird on the phone before"

"Did I?" stalling for time, trying to think.

"Yes you know you did"

"I was just a bit worried. I'd rung you a few times and my mind started working overtime when you didn't answer"

"Working overtime about what?"

"I don't know... that the baby might have arrived early or you might've had a car crash or I don't know"

"Oh Sammy, you are daft" she laughs as she takes a sip of her glass of tonic water. I just smile as best I can and tuck into my soup. It's tastes as good as it smells. Better even. Like a million tiny orgasms on your tongue and I go at it like a bull in a china shop. I drain the bowl but refrain from having seconds as I want to save room for my main.

Just as I'm about to tuck into my deep fried shredded chilli chicken, there's a rapid knock at the door and my heart attempts to leave my body via my throat. The concern is clear on my face and she can see it plain as day.

"I'll get it" I tell her as I leap up from the table a little too quickly.

"Sammy what's the matter?" she asks me with an anxious edge to her voice.

"Nothing babe" I tell her as I go to the front door.

Who will it be? Could this be the one? The unwelcome visitor? The call that ends my cosy little world?

I approach the door with caution and peek through the window at the side but it's no good. Whoever it is, is stood too far over and all I can see is their shadow.

There's only one way to face this and that's to just open the door and take whatever's waiting for me. My heart is racing as I place my hand on the latch and turn.

"Now then!" I almost leap from my skin as Alfie greets me with his usual enthusiasm.

"Alright kidder" Relief isn't the word.

"Bloody hell Sam, you alright la? You look the colour of boiled shite"

"No I'm fine la, I'm fine" I'm far from fine.

"Fancy a couple over the Coey?" he enquires

"Amy's cooked us a meal mate"

"Ah, no problems la, say no more" and with that, he's off.

"See you later" he bids me as he wanders off down the path.

I've known Alfie since I can remember and he lives three doors down. He's all day. Top notch. The kind of fella you can trust with your life and the way things are going that might just be the case.

I saunter back through and plonk myself down at the table.

"Sammy, what the hell is going on?" she asks, her face a mask of apprehension.

"What?" Not the best reply, but time is of the essence.

"What do you mean what? You nearly jumped off the chair when the door went, that's not normal behaviour is it?"

"Sorry babe, I'm just really tired that's all, I haven't had a day off in six months what with the doors and that have I?"

"Well no but, you looked terrified Sam, really terrified. Is there something I should know?"

There's the sixty four thousand dollar question. Is there something she should know? There's quite a lot of things she probably should know but it would mean the end of life as we know it and that can't happen.

"There's nothing babe, honestly" A change of subject is required here "Anyway, never mind all that now. You haven't got anything planned for the next week have you?"

"I don't think so why?"

"We're all going to stay in a log cabin in the lakes"

"We are?" this has thrown her.

"Yep, booked it today, the place looks amazing"

"Aren't we a bit far out in case anything happens" she says as she motions towards the large bump in her stomach.

"No that's the thing. We're only a few miles from the local hospital. It's perfect"

The smile spreads across her face and lights up the room. Safe again, for now.

CHAPTER 38

THE CABIN IS TRULY AMAZING and the kids love it. We spend our days relaxing, playing games and enjoying the clement spring weather. I've always loved the spring. It's my favourite season. I love the smells and the colours and the promise of things to come.

I occasionally manage to slip away and phone Terry and as far as he knows, things are still ok. No one has come looking for us yet.

Alfie is keeping an eye on the house and everything's fine there as well. No news is good news I suppose. I'm managing to relax myself, but it still hits me now and again. The thought that all this could come crashing down around my ears still haunts me. I sit and watch my beautiful family laughing and smiling and the thought that I have put all this in jeopardy makes me sick to my gut. We may be financially secure but I'd rather not have a pot to piss in for the rest of our lives than put all this at risk. But it's too late now isn't it? The die is cast, the deed is done and now all I can do is wait to see which way it all lands.

If I could go back and change things, I would. I would tell Terry not to be so daft and fob the whole idea off. I really would, no two ways about it. I've had time to think and I've come to the conclusion that I've made a monumental mistake.

My mind keeps flicking to the stash of money in the workshop and instead of filling me with a warm glow as it has done, it now makes me feel sick. It is a constant reminder of what I've done, of how low I've sunk. I am a murderer. A cold blooded one at that.

I am vulnerable. There's people that know too much. Rodney for example. What other connections does he have in Liverpool's fair city? Will he have remarked at the quality and cost of our product to others? He's only a few miles away right now. It would be so easy just to slip away for an hour or two and tie up business there wouldn't it?

And how much has Terry told this Finchy? More than he's letting on? Who can tell? Must get the lad's address. Know thine enemy. Keep them close. Can't let anyone be the fly in the ointment. Got to keep it all together, eggs in one basket, keep it tight.

Maybe Rodney would be pleased to hear from me? Nice of him to give me his number. Be rude not to drop in when I'm only round the corner. I'll text Alfie to ring me tonight, use the call as cover.

The phone is in my hand and I'm dialling the number without mentally opting to do so. It rings four times then is answered by that monotone Brummie accent.

"Hello?"

"Rodney! It's Sammy, how you doin'?"

"Foin Sam thanks for askin' and yow?"

"Very Good Rodney, very good. Are you around tomorrow only there's something I need to come and see you about, six things I need to come and see you about actually"

"That sounds spot on that does Sam, Tirroye comin' with yow?"

"No, just me good self, Terry's on a bit of a sabbatical at the mo' if you know what I mean"

"Roight, yeah, no problems Sammy"

"Twelve alright for you?"

"That'll do noicely"

"See you then"

Too easy.

Chapter 39

We're just relaxing, watching telly and my phone goes. Alfie lad you're a fucking star.

"Hello?" I answer, face a picture of confusion.

"Alright la it's me" Alfie's voice comes quietly through the earpiece.

"Hiya Frank what's up?"

"Ah, one of these is it?" Alfie asks.

I leave it for a few moments longer and reply

"Tomorrow? Can't anyone else go?"

"What the fuck are you up to?" Alfie laughs down my ear.

"Well I suppose I could, hang on a mo" I reply and I cover the phone with my hand and turn to Amy "It's Frank, the client in Keswick wants to tie up a few loose ends of the contract and he wants me to go. Would you mind if I slope off for an hour or two tomorrow?"

She looks at me, head on one side with a wry smile "Of course I don't mind. You're not going to be all day though are you?"

"No, no should only take a couple of hours at the most"

"Fine, me and the kids will just have to entertain ourselves until you get back" she jokes.

I put the phone back to my ear "Ok Frank, just this once, but you owe me"

"I don't know what the fuck you're doing but good luck" Alfie says, completely puddled.

"Yeah, you too"

The groundwork is set. The deception is complete. I am scum.

CHAPTER 40

DRIVING TOWARDS KESWICK, I'M WONDERING how I'm going to do it. I don't have a gun and no possible way of getting hold of one in the immediate future. That leaves sharp weapons, blunt weapons or bare hands.

I can't believe I'm actually having this dilemma. I'm driving down one of the most picturesque roads in this or any other country and I'm agonising over how I'm going to end somebody's life. The thing is, I've got to know by the time I get there. Uncertainty and improvisation could tip the scales very much against me, and I've only got a small window in which to do the deed.

This is very different than the others. They were all spontaneous, spare of the moment things. I acted, or reacted to the situation as it unfolded without a thought of the consequences. It was only later, when the adrenalin had left my system and reality had returned that I got chance to assess all that had gone on.

This is very, very different though. This really is cold blooded shit. Hello Rodney, Bang! Goodnight Vienna. Is that how it will go? Will it be that simple? The dopey sod won't have an inkling that there will be any skulduggery will he? Mellow as fuck he is. That's another thing, I quite like the soft twat. Fucking nice that isn't it? Just fucking perfect. Would it be any easier if he was a prick? I haven't got a clue, to be honest, is the answer to that one.

Right now I haven't got a clue about anything. My mind is closing in. Must be panic taking control.

Focus Sammy lad for fuck's sake.

However I do it, I can't spill too much blood. Can't afford to get it on my clothes as I don't have any spare, so I think a blunt instrument would be best. Swift blow to the back of the head should do it. The thing is though, I'm going to have to make sure he's dead aren't I? If the cunt wakes up with nothing more than a migraine there's going to be consequences isn't there? So how do I make sure he's a goner? Check his pulse? Fucking Dr. Crippin here eh? I can just see me feeling around his wrist or neck and looking at my watch. What am I fucking thinking about here?

I pull the car over to the side of the road and rest my head on the steering wheel.

Right Sammy lad. If you've ever pulled your tripe out before, this is the time to do it and make it a good'un.

Think. Heavy object. Sounds a bit clichéd but the wheel brace in the boot should do the trick. Nice and concealable. I'll put it in the bag I'm taking with me. After all, it'd look a bit suss if I turn up to sell him a load of bugle with nothing on me wouldn't it? I've put a few bits and pieces in the bag to make it look like there's something in it. I'll pretend I'm pulling the gear out of the bag and instead I'll be pulling out steely death for Mr. Rodney... I don't even know the cunt's second name. And what that's got to do with anything I don't know, it just seems a little callous, doing the lad over and I don't know his surname. Why the fuck should it matter? Not a prerequisite of the job is it? Not an essential part of the murderer/victim relationship really.

I've got to think disposal. This is where preplanning is an advantage. I have time to prepare. Fire seems to be the best option. After all, it's worked fine before. Get rid of everything, that's the best way. I'll fill the plastic petrol container up at the next garage. A few carefully placed matches and the whole thing should be one glorious conflagration.

The good thing about Rodney's gaff is that the front door isn't overlooked. Nice anonymous entrance and exit. No interference, no unwanted attention. Happy days.

The thought hasn't escaped me that there's going to be a considerable amount of cash here as well and I can't just leave it behind can I? That would be fucking stupid now wouldn't it? I'll have to take it with me. Fuck knows what I'm going to do with it though. I'll have to cross that bridge when I come to it. Think about it on the way back. Right now I've got to focus on the job in hand… which is killing some poor fucker who really doesn't deserve it. But I can't think like that can I? This is just another precaution to make sure things run smoothly for me and my family and that's how I've got to keep looking at it. It's just a job, that's all. Just a job. Just a means to an end. Keeping my house in order so to speak. And it has to be done. No two ways about it. It has to be done. He won't feel a thing. Hopefully. God I hope he doesn't. I'll have to make it swift and accurate. Straight to the back of his head as hard as I can. Best roll my sleeves up first. Don't want any claret on my clobber now do I? Have you heard me? Claret? I sound like a frustrated cockney.

Mind's racing again now, slow down Sammy lad, slow down. Cool, calm and collected. Just think about the hitmen in the movies. They're always super cool aren't they? Emotionless, expressionless, deadly. And they'd be psychopaths as well, wouldn't they? Cold hearted, sociopathic, killers for whom killing is no more dramatic than making a cup of tea. Not the best train of thought there Sam. Not the best way to approach this. Just try and relax and let everything go from your mind, a kind of Zen approach if you like. Like this is all not real. This is all the dream of Buddha or some other spiritual icon.

I've completely lost the plot now. What the fuck am I going on about now? Hitmen? Buddha? For fuck's sake!

Get a grip. Be a man. Be strong, if not for yourself then for your family. Think about what it will mean to them to have you around and alive for a bit longer. What would it do to them if you were to be bumped off? The question has to be asked, what would the powers that be do to them after I was bumped off? Would it end with me or would they make an example and go after Amy and the kids? After all, we have stepped on some pretty heavy toes. Since all that palaver with Tommy Monaghan being shot, the Buck's have been the major force in the city and haven't they let people know about it.

And we've killed Billy Buck's nephew and Jerry Jacobs's bag man who ultimately will have been working for Billy, once you get to the top of the chain of command.

All this adds up to a big payback. A payback of monstrous proportions.

All it will take is for JJ to work out who fired the gun and we're in the mire up to our necks anyway.

Apparently, the bizzies have matched the casing found at the home of the steg head and the bullet that was found inside him, with the box that was found when they raided that other dealers gaff as well, so that's going to throw them all off the scent for a while at least.

I could just turn around now and go back to Amy and the kids. Phone Rodney and tell him it's a no-no. I could forget about the whole fucked up idea.

I could, but I'm not going to...

CHAPTER 41

"Hello Sammy, how're yow doin'?"

"Fine thanks Rodney, just fine"

He invites me inside. Bad move.

"Oi didn't expect yow after the last lot" he informs me "Oi thought yow said youm were retoirin'?"

"Had a change of plan mate" I tell him, trying to keep the stress from my voice "This lot came along and I couldn't say no"

"Makes sense doesn't it?" Rodney nods.

"Yeah, yeah" Fuck this is getting difficult.

"Let's have a look at the gear then" he tells me "That last lot raised a few eyebrows loike so I'd loike to test this lot if yow don't moind?"

"Eh? Yeah… no problem Rodney… no problem"

"Yow alright Sam? Yow look at bit out of sorts there mate"

"No, I'm fine … just a bit tired… been working long hours and that haven't I? You got the money?"

"Of course Oi have. Why wouldn't Oi?"

He's getting suspicious now. Not badly but he's aware that all is not well.

"Just asking kidder, that's all"

"Come on then, let the dog see the rabbit"

"Right" I reply. This is it. The moment of truth. The final hour. Shit or bust.

I delve my hand into the bag and my fingers close around the cold steel of my intended murder weapon. Rodney's watching me, stood just out of striking distance. This is all wrong. He should be facing the other way. I should have engineered the situation better. Should have taken charge from the off. Instead I've let things run their course and they've tumbled out of my control. He's stood there, watching, waiting, seeing. My hand starts to move out of the bag. Slowly. Deliberately. No going back. No way out. Only one direction to go. Can't delay anymore. His eagerness to get down to business is going to cost him precious seconds of his limited life. Nothing I can do.

My hand comes free of the bag and realisation hits him the instant he sees what's in my hand.

"Sammy! No!" He almost screams "Why?"

I move towards him with as much speed as I can muster and he backs away towards the wall, terror gripping his features.

Now Sammy lad, strike now, but something's stopping me. Holding me back. Can't bring myself to swing the ultimate blow.

"On your knees" I tell him. Stalling for time. Trying to conjure the necessary will power and strength needed to do what I've got to do.

He drops to the floor on his hands and knees and looks up into my face beseechingly.

"Why Sammy? What I have done to deserve this? I've always paid youm well haven't I?"

"Shut up, shut the fuck up" I spit at him. The last thing I need is him pleading for his life.

Shit! Shit! Shit! This is bad. This is very bad. Just do it Sammy lad, just do it. Swing the fucking wheel brace and let's get the fuck out of here. Come on for fuck's sake. Think. The sooner you do this, the sooner you can get back to Amy and the kids. The sooner you can carry on with your family time together. This has to be done. To ensure your safety, this has to be done. No way out. Not now. You could have just walked away five minutes ago before you knocked on the door though. Five minutes ago you had options. Now you don't. Now there's only one thing you can do. You're in a blind alley, facing a dead end. There really is only one thing you can do.

I raise the weapon above my head and go to bring it down with as much force as I can but I'm halted by the sound of Rodney sobbing.

"For fuck's sake Rodney, pack it in will you?" I tell him weakly but he just continues, the tears rolling down the bridge of his nose and dropping off the end.

"Please Sammy, don't kill me, please" he begs and the urge to spew the contents of my stomach nearly wins.

"Yow can have it all" he tells me "There's three hundred grand and four kilos here and yow can have it all just take it and Oi won't say a word to anyone Oi promise yow, Sammy, Oi really promise yow" his last words are nearly lost in amongst his tears.

"You know I can't do that" I tell him through clenched teeth. All the time trying to keep my own emotions contained for as long as I can.

His crying escalates now and he grabs my shins and pleads for mercy. I try and step back but he won't let go. He's literally hugging my lower legs now, so frantic are his pleas and there's snot and tears all over my kecks.

"Rodney get the fuck off" I tell him.

"No Sammy, No. Yow don't have to do this, yow really don't. Please God no. Please!"

"Get the fuck off!" but again he just holds tighter.

"Rodney for fuck's sake, get your hands off" and before I know it, I've swung the wheel brace and the sound of sobbing has ceased. The pressure on my lower legs has given way and all is calm for a moment.

The wheel brace is a deep crimson. The sound it made when it connected with his skull was indescribable. Sickening doesn't even come close. The saliva, tears and snot on my trousers have been overlaid with my victim's blood and it's everywhere. All up my legs, on my hands, on my face. Everywhere. It's like there's been an explosion in a blood bank. How can so much blood come from one blow? This is fucking ridiculous. Outrageous. Un-fucking-believable.

I stand amongst the carnage I have created and survey my handy work and that's enough as far as my stomach is concerned. It's entire contents come cascading through my mouth like a Technicolor fountain, spraying the surrounding area and my victim with foul smelling vomit. Charming. Just another substance to add to the conglomeration on my clothing.

This is bad. This is very bad. I'm a rancid mess. A putrid, fetid mess. What the fuck am I going to do now? I can't exactly go back to the cabin like this can I? I look like Hannibal Lector after a good meal.

There's only one thing for it, I'm going to have to wash my clothes in Rodney's washing machine and dry them in his tumble dryer so we are talking a good couple of hours here, maybe three. I'll just have to ring Amy and tell her that the meeting's going on a bit longer, that's all. She'll understand. I'll leave it a while though, til I've calmed down a bit. If I ring her now she'll know for certain something's up.

What the fuck am I going to do for three hours in a strange house with a rapidly cooling corpse? Watch telly? Fuck that.

CHAPTER 42

JUST OVER AN HOUR HAS gone by and my nerves are starting to settle.

I've phoned Amy and although she sounded a bit pissed off, I think she'll be fine.

My clothes are on the final rinse and I'm sitting here in my undercrackers next to a corpse of my own creation, waiting for god knows who to come through the front door.

I've fastened all the locks and put a chair up against the handle, but somehow it doesn't feel enough. I've never felt more vulnerable in my life. My ultimate freedom depends on the speed of a domestic appliance.   How fucking De Niro is that? You see hitmen in the films who do the job then get the fuck out of there tout suite. They don't sit around in their bills reading Angling Times. That's the only literature I can find by the way, fucking Angling Times. I daren't switch the telly on in case anyone does come to the door and hears it. Might raise a few suspicions and I want to leave nothing to chance.

This is fucking ridiculous this is. Absolutely fucking stupid. I should be long gone. Down the road. Far away and safe. Instead I'm sitting here like a lemon.

I pull the petrol canister out of the bag and place it on the table. At least this will cover all tracks. This will cleanse the place of any evidence leading to me. I can't wait to soak the place, strike the match and get the fuck out of here.

I sit back down and as I stare at Rodney's corpse it groans and I jump a foot in the air.

Fuck! Shit! The twat's not dead! For fuck's sake this is all I need.

I leap up and frantically search for the wheel brace but I can't find it. Where the fuck have I put it now? Jesus Christ Sammy you fucking dozy prick, where the fuck is it?

Rodney's starting to move now, trying to lift himself up on his elbows. Where is that fucking wheel brace? I'm going through the room like a dose of salts but it's nowhere to be seen. Think Sammy, think. What did you do with it after you'd finished before? I'm sure I put it on the table, I'm almost positive. But it's not there now. Definitely.

I scour the room for something else to use and come up with very little. In an instant I'm into the kitchen.

The third draw down produces a suitable looking knife and I dash back into the front room to find Rodney three foot from where I committed the previous atrocity, trying to make it to the door. He looks so pathetic and again I pause before I deliver the capital blow.

Come on Sammy, you've done it before, just do the same again, just stick him with it. But it's so very difficult. The groaning has turned into a mutated form of sobbing now and the sound is tearing at my heartstrings.

If this fella had harmed Amy or the kids I would have no problem doing this. Truth is I'd probably relish it, but this? This is positively sick. The poor lad's done fuck all and I'm putting him through this.

The humane thing to do would be to put him out of his misery, I know. The pain he'll be feeling must be excruciating. The terror and the horror, I can only guess, must be unbearable.

That's it Sammy, this will now be a mercy killing won't it? Taking the lad out of a desperate situation. It'll be for the best.

I'm surprised at how easily the knife slides into the side of his neck. Like the proverbial hot knife through butter. His body tenses for a second or two, then thankfully goes limp and comes to rest at a bizarre angle on the floor.

Taking the knife out, however is a different matter and I have to put my foot on the side of his head to gain enough leverage. It eventually glides out to the accompaniment of a rather disgusting 'shlupp' sound. Again, there's blood everywhere, but this time it doesn't matter so much. This time there's no clothes, socks or shoes to cover, just bare feet.

Just to be on the safe side I plunge the blade back in the other side of his neck and again I have to wrench it out. If the cunt's not dead now he'd want to be.

Again the feeling of extreme nausea hits me but there's nothing left in my aching stomach to expel, so I stand there dry retching, tiny flecks of bile adorning my contorted face. What a fucking mess?

When eventually the convulsing subsides, I fall onto the couch, gripping my tormented guts, waiting for the pain to subside. It truly is agony. It's the same pain I've been getting for quite a while now, only magnified a hundred times. I keep meaning to go to the quack's about it but I can never seem to find the time and anyway, what would I tell him? 'Yes Doc, the pain is usually worse right after I've killed somebody' don't fucking think so. It'll subside in a bit, it usually does. If anyone were to barge their way into the house now I would be powerless to do anything. I couldn't even lift the knife again the pain's that bad.

Come on Sammy lad, ride the pain, you can do it. Just keep your head up, relax, let it drain away. I know that the longer my mind is in turmoil, the longer the pain will stay, so I need to calm down and let it all go, which is easier said than done when there's a bloodied and battered corpse not six feet from you.

Come on now Sammy, think of the money. Think of all that lovely dough. I've searched the place as well, by the way, and Rodney was true to his word. There was a considerable bundle of cash which looks very much like it will be at least three hundred grand and I've also found the four bags of beak which leaves me with two quandaries: How do I stash the cash and do I take the bugle or leave it behind? One thing's for fucking certain, the cash is coming with me. That is a definite. If anything's to come out of this it might as well be financial. Fuck knows how I'm going to get it home but that's a different matter.

What would I do with the coke if I took it? There was only one person I knew who would take it off my hands and I've just killed him. I can't tell Terry about it, there'd be too many questions and he's not stupid. Once news spreads of Rodney's demise he'll put two and two together quicker than Stephen Hawkins.

Do I know anyone else? Is it worth the risk? In monetary terms I'm looking at another hundred grand or thereabouts and that's still a lot of money.

What would I do with it though? I can't take it back to the cabin with me, that would just be plain fucking stupid. I can't exactly post it anywhere can I? Could I find anywhere around here to stash it in the limited time I've got? And if I take it with me and can't find anywhere to stash it, how do I destroy it then? It'll have my prints and DNA all over it won't it? At least if I leave it here it'll go up in flames with everything else.

If there was someone I could trust to pick it up I'd be sorted. Someone who wouldn't question what I'm doing and would back me all the way. Someone who's all day.

Alfie! Fucking top notch idea. He'd be well up for it and I know I could trust him with my life, which might not be very far from the mark the way things are going.

The pain's starting to give way now and my thoughts are clearing. I'm starting to see the positive side to this now and that can only be a good thing. Financially speaking, this hasn't been a bad day. Not a bad day at all.

I wander through to the kitchen to find that the washing machine has finally finished it's cycle. I try to open the door and panic hits me when it doesn't move. Shit! My clothes are trapped. What the fuck am I going to do now? Then it hits me. The time lock, that's all it is, the fucking time lock and anyway, if they were trapped I could've just kicked the door open couldn't I? It's not as if any of this is going to be here in an hour or two is it? Sometimes I just don't think past a certain point.

There's an almost inaudible click and I open the door and transfer all my clothes into the dryer, quickly checking them over as I do so. At first glance it doesn't look like there's any stains but I'll have to give them a thorough going over once they're dry. I'm on the home straight now.

I go back through to the front room, pick my phone up off the side and dial Alfie's number.

"Now then" comes his cheerful greeting after three rings.

"Alright kidder, how's it going?"

"Sound la, sound. Enjoying the holiday?"

"Oh aye, very relaxing" I lie.

"The house is fine" he tells me "No problems and I've been walking the dog"

"Nice one. Listen, I need you to do me a favour"

"What's that?" he enquires.

"I need you to pick a package up for me up here in the lakes, only it's not all above board, if you catch my drift"

"I knew you was up to something you rapscallion you" he jokes. Wonder if he'll be joking when he looks in the bag?

"There's a nice bit of wedge in it for you of course" I tell him

"Oh yeah? How much?"

"Well it's not Brewster's but it'll do"

"Only kiddin' la. Of course I'll do it. I was only jokin' about the dosh, I'm not arsed am I?" he laughs.

"Nice one. I'll bell you when I know the exact location, but it's going to have to be tonight, that ok?"

"Fuckin' hell la, talk about short notice"

"I know but this is the only opportunity I have, d'you get me?"

"Not exactly la, no"

"You will"

"Alright then mate, no bother. Just let me know as soon as you can and I'll be up. You're gonna have to give us a bit of dosh for petrol though cos I'm fuckin' skint at the mo"

"No problems, I'll leave you a bit in the bag and I'll give you the rest when I get home, that alright?"

"Spot on la"

"Nice one. I'll bell you when I know then ok?"

"Sound, speak to you later"

He's a fucking legend is Alfie. Absolute, hundred and ten percent, out and out legend. I'll give him fifty grand for this, after all, that's half the price of the gear isn't it? It's only fair. He'll be made up with that.

Now, what to do with the mergunney? I don't want to put that in the bag for Alfie as well. It's not that I don't trust him, just that I don't want to put all my eggs in one basket, know what I mean? Doesn't make sense. If the package is compromised, then all we'll lose is the gear and a couple of quid. Three hundred bag of sand is too much to lose at one sitting I'm sure you'll agree.

Time for a shower. Got to remove any trace of all of this nastiness. Got to get cleaned up, ready to leave when my clothes are done.

I'm on my way up the stairs and there's a knock at the door. It had to happen didn't it? Sod's fucking law. I freeze where I stand and wait. After a few moments, the knock comes again only this time it's louder and more rapid.

The letterbox flips open and a voice comes floating through.

"Rodney, it's Baz, you in there?"

Luckily, there's no window in the door, so I creep back down the stairs, pick up the blood stained knife and secrete myself in a suitable position behind the door to spring should the need arise.

"Rodney open the door man. I know I'm a bit late but I'm here now aren't I? Come on for fuck's sake"

There must have been and pre-arranged rendezvous. This isn't good.

"Fine, I'll just get the keys from under the mat then" The voice informs me. Shit! Shit! Shit! This is bad. This is very bad. I whip the chair away from under the handle and wait, knife clutched in hand, coiled like a cobra, ready to spring. Not another one, please god not another one. I don't think my guts can take it.

The sound of the first lock rolling back makes my stomach roll with it. I know there's three and the second follows close behind. Here we go. Bollocks, fucking bollocks I can't stand this. My head's going to explode. My veins are going to burst out of my neck. My skin is on fire. I'm at the brink of death myself, I must be. I'm going to burst any minute. This is it. My heart can't keep up this pace, I am a dead man.

The handle turns but the door doesn't move.

"What the fuck's he put the dead bolt on for?" I here the disembodied voice mumble to it's self. Thank fuck! Thank fuck for that, I remember now, the third lock was indeed a dead bolt. No way of opening that from the outside is there?" Fucking marvellous. Tremendous. Remarkable.

"Fuck you then" comes the voice again "I'll go to Burnsy instead in future if you're gonna be a moody twat about it" Can't be certain but I'm sure there's a hint of a scouse accent there. Daft prick doesn't know how close he came to being shivved.

I collapse on the floor and wait for my breathing to calm down. My heart is pounding in my chest and my head is banging. Got to get the fuck out of here, if I stay much longer I'm going to have a stroke.

I eventually get up and go to the kitchen to check on my clothes, carefully observing Rodney on the way. I know the fucker's dead but after last time I'm not taking any chances. But he doesn't move as I pass by.

My clothes are still damp. Only another fifteen or twenty minutes left, surely.

Each minute is dragging now, stretching out into hours, decades even. I'm so close to getting out of here. So close.

I have a shower and after a quick scan around, I find a bag belonging to the householder and proceed to fill it with the packets of devil's dandruff. I fill my own bag with the cash and wrap the knife up in a tea towel. Only one thing remains now and that's the wheel brace. Where the fuck have I put it? It's got to be here somewhere. It can't have got up and walked so where the fuck is it? This is starting to make me panic again and I can feel the tension rising in my chest. Right. Let's think about this logically. I twatted him over the head with it, he slumped to the floor, then I'm sure I put it on the table just before or after I puked. I can't be sure which. But it's definitely not there now is it?

The penny drops and I lift the bag to reveal the offending article. Thank fuck for that! What a wanker? My mind is like a sieve. How obvious was that? It's lapses in concentration like that that's going to get me hung.

I quickly wrap it in the tea towel with the knife and place the pair in the bag. Got to dispose of them properly. If I've learnt anything from the telly it's the importance of disposing of the murder weapon. Thankyou Miss Marple, Hercule Poirot and CSI.

I open the dryer door and check my clothes again. Not long now. Very nearly done. Everything's ready to go, just need my clobber and I'm away.

I pick the petrol can up off the table and begin liberally distributing it around the front room and the kitchen. I slosh some inside the washing machine to make sure it goes up properly. Don't want to leave any fibres now do I Horatio? I'll do the same to the dryer once my clothes are finished. Can't be long now.

After a few minutes I check them again and they're dry enough. I dress as quickly as possible, sluice the dryer with petrol, sling the bags over my back and pour a trail of petrol to the front door. After a couple of minutes of fumbling with the locks, I'm outside on the porch, matches in hand. I take a couple of steps back, strike a match and throw it towards the trail of petrol and nothing happens. The match just goes dead on the floor. That's not how it happens in the films is it? I strike another, lash it and the same happens. Bollocks. This is not how things are supposed to go. In my frustration I light another and thrust it inside the box, igniting the rest of the matches and hurl it inside. The flames burst before the matchbox even touches the floor. With an almost deafening Whump, the place goes up like an incendiary device and almost knocks me on my arse.

I stagger back slightly and instinctively check my eyebrows, but they're still in tact. If I were any closer I reckon I would have a lot of explaining to do when I eventually get back to the cabin. But all's well and the house is blazing. This is no time to stand around and admire my handiwork so I'm off on my toes, out of the drive and away down the street with a bag slung over each shoulder. I've parked the car a few streets away for safety and I'm inside with the engine running within minutes. Got to stay calm though. Can't go screaming off, even though the urge to do so is almost irresistible, don't want to raise any suspicions.

I cruise slowly out of the street and onto the main road in the direction of Derwent Water and the further away I get, the more I relax.

That has got to be the worst three hours of my entire fucking life. No comparison. That was horrendous. I never want to have to go through anything like that again, ever. I'm physically shaking now. I think shock is taking it's toll and I have to pull the car over and sit for a while. After a few minutes the tears start to well in my eyes and in seconds I'm crying like a baby. Wailing even. I'm sobbing so hard that I'm struggling to catch my breath. How much more of this can I take before I completely lose my marbles? It seems like a never ending road, like I've opened up some kind of Pandora's box that's not going to go back together no matter what I try and do to stop it. It just keeps opening and opening and it's getting way out of my control. How many more will have to die before I'm safe? How many more atrocities will I have to commit before this whole sordid episode comes to a close? I know for a fact that this is far from over and the weight of it is almost crushing me.

Come on Sammy lad pull yourself together. You're on the home straight now. The hard bit's done. Don't fall to pieces now, just calm down and breathe slowly. That's it, nice and peaceful, nice and settled, that's it. Think of Amy. Think of the kids. You can't let them down now can you? Not when you've come this far. It'd be plain fucking stupid to let it all go now wouldn't it? Fucking right it would. Just breathe, that's it, breathe. Wipe your face, put the car in gear and let's finish this properly eh?   Fucking right. This is nearly done and dusted, just the last fence to jump, the last bridge to cross, the last hurdle to overcome and it's done... for now anyway.

The car moves off at a snail's pace and I bimble down the road in the direction of the lake.

The next step is to find a suitable stash place to hide the gear, but not so good as Alfie can't find it. It's got to be on the banks of the lake, it has to be. That's got to be the best place, it's just finding a spot where there's no tourists.

I follow the road to Stonethwaite once more and I can't help thinking that the last time I travelled this way, it was under much more jovial circumstances.

After a couple of minutes I spot the place. Nice and secluded, but easily recognisable from the road. This has got to be it.

I park the car off the road and in seconds I've got the bag from the boot and I'm off and walking. No-one around. No-one at all. This is perfect. The bag isn't that big and thankfully it's a dark brown colour, so it won't stick out like a blind cobbler's thumb. I look inside just to check, even though I know it's all there: Four bags of white poison and five grand in cash. That should be enough for Alfie for now. I'm sure that'll buy him enough petrol to get him back home. Like I said, I'll weigh him in properly when I get home. He's a family man himself is Alfie, but he's no angel, or he wasn't in the past. In our glory days he consumed a fair amount of class A's himself and he's not exactly naïve to the benefits of knocking it out. He'll be sound. No problem there.

I take out the tea towel, unwrap the knife and wheel brace and launch them as far as I can into the lake. Another loose end tied up and I walk on.

The perfect spot springs up on me and my shoulders sag with the relief. A large tree, with a kind of hollow trunk screams 'over here' at me. It's not far from a bench so will be easily identifiable. Bang on.

I wedge the bag in and it fits perfectly. Once I've rearranged some of the surrounding foliage, you'd never know it was there.

The last piece of the jigsaw now is to inform Alfie of the where-abouts and I'm done for the day. Clocking off time.

I pull my phone out of my pocket but there's no signal. I'll call him on the way back to the cabin. But that's it for now though. All over red rover. My body feels like it's been in a cement mixer and my head feels like a bowl of soup. But it's done. That's the main thing. It's done. And didn't he do well? A round of applause for the winning contestant please. Three cheers for the returning hero... hip hip!

CHAPTER 43

BACK AT THE CABIN, I'M drained and Amy can see it.

"You ok babe?" she asks, voice laden with concern.

"Yeah, I'm fine" I lie "Just a bit tired, that's all. How're you more to the point?"

"Oh, I'm ok"

"No signs of anything stirring yet?" I ask as I gesture towards her distended stomach.

"Apart from the little bugger trying to kick me to death from the inside, no"

"Good stuff" I reply as I lean over and kiss the swelling under her tee shirt. I turn my head to one side and listen to the faint churning and swilling noises coming from her abdomen and the sound is hypnotic. She places her hand on my head and strokes my hair and I'm asleep in minutes.

CHAPTER 44

I KNOW I'M DREAMING. THIS is obvious, such is the surreal world I am moving through. Nothing makes sense. Nothing fits. Sounds, sights, colours, textures, faces, people, lakes, bags, money, petrol, fire, blood, urine, faeces, flies, rats, decay, screams, trees, screams, benches, screams, money.

The sound of screaming is drowning everything else out now, so loud and sharp. So shrill, it feels like it's going to burst my eardrums.

Hands. I can feel hands on me. Shaking me. Slapping me. Holding me. Almost hurting me. Increasing my panic. Bolstering my fear. More screams. Louder, harsher, filled with horror. Hands all over me. Shaking. Frantic. Frenzied. Terror. Shear terror. Gripping. Throttling. Suffocating terror. No escape. No way out. Louder, louder. Piercing. Painful. Hurtful. Voices, louder. Voices, familiar. Voices, terrified. No way out. No way back. No way forward. Stuck in time in this very second. This is torture. This is hell. Nothing would be better. Nothing would be best.

Faces. Familiar faces. Shocked faces. Frightened faces. Friendly faces. My faces. Their faces. Our faces. Family. Close. Nearly there. Very close. Can almost touch them. Can almost feel them. Can't let go. Not now. Not right now. Got to keep them with me. Got to hold on to them. Keep them close. Keep them safe. Keep them sheltered. Clearer, sharper, with me. Still with me. Thank god they're still with me. Must keep on though. Got to keep on. Can't stop. Mustn't stop. Tight chest. Pains. Shooting pains. Frightening pains. Faces! Keep them with me. Don't go. Not now. Not yet. Stay a while longer. Keep me company. Keep me together. Keep me sane. Keep me warm. Keep me. Can't remember me. Can't remember. Can't recall. Anything. Can't keep it. Can't keep me. Faces! Keep the faces. Keep them with me. Keep them close.

CHAPTER 45

As I REGAIN CONSCIOUSNESS I'm alarmed to discover that the screaming is coming from me. From my own mouth.

Amy and the kids are surrounding me stricken with fear. Terrified at the performance I'm putting on. I leap from the couch and only just make it in time to the toilet before the contents of my stomach make their second appearance of the day.

I retch and retch long after the last piece of undigested food comes up and at one point I think the lining of my stomach is going to come up to greet me.

Amy's behind me with her hand rubbing my back and words of comfort. I'm okay. I'm fine. I'm back in reality, back to sanity.

That was bizarre. That was really fucking bizarre. I can still feel some residual pain in my left shoulder and this begins to worry me until I remember that I was lying on my left side and the pain I am feeling is probably just pins and needles. Of course it is. I'm only thirty five, for fuck's sake, I'm hardly going to be having a heart attack am I?

The retching has subsided now and I'm able to stand up straight. The kids are crying, such is their terror at their old man's behaviour and I do my best to assuage them.

"Hey you two, what's all this about?" I ask them in my calmest possible voice "Daddy was just having a bad dream, that's all. No need to worry"

Amy runs up and throws her arms around my waist.

"Why are you being sick then? I never be sick when I have a nightmare"

"I must've eaten something that hasn't agreed with me sweetheart, but I'm alright now"

The little fella, seeing that all has now returned to normality, comes up and hugs my legs too and I'm pinned where I stand by my two beautiful children and my wife as she hugs me as well. We stand there for a couple of minutes, locked in our mutual embrace. A complete family. *My* complete family. The loving family of a monster. I'm like a comic book villain; a paradox between loving caring family man and cold blooded killer. I am truly not worthy of this.

Rodney's face swims up in my mind. The beseeching look in his eyes. The sobs and pleas for his life.

Don't do this to yourself Sammy lad. You did what you had to do, end of. Now get on with the rest of your holiday with your amazing family and get on with the rest of your life and if anyone else gets in the way of that well... well what? You'll slot them as well? Add a couple more to the death toll? Why not? They're only scum after all. Just a smear on society, pedalling misery and death to millions. It's not as if they're innocents is it? Is it fuck? They're all scum. I've never killed anyone who's not involved in this sordid little world have I? Rodney might've been a nice fella but he was still a dealer in various poisons wasn't he? A large scale dealer at that. I've probably cut the supply to the Lake District by a considerable amount. So in that respect, you could say I'm a bit of a vigilante and not a comic book villain after all, rather a comic book hero. Anti Drug Man! Here to fight the forces of evil. Incorruptible, virtuous and strong.

So you're not going to sell the four kilos that Alfie picked up last night then?

Shut up.

Chapter 46

THE NEXT MORNING, I'M UP early and off for a walk down to the local shop for a paper and some milk. On the way I phone Alfie and after four rings he answers.

"Easy Geezer" he greets me with a decidedly upbeat tone.

"Now then, everything go okay?"

"Fuckin' spot on la, absolutely spot on"

"Good stuff, good stuff. You've got it stashed nice and safe then?" I ask.

"Oh aye kidder. Safe as houses"

"Nice one and you got the money?"

"Yeah, I thought you said you weren't gonna' put it all in"

"I didn't"

"What? There's more?" He asks incredulously.

"Oh aye mate. It was only five grand wasn't it?"

"Only? Fuckin' hell la Five grand's plenty for me. That'll well pull me out of the mire that will"

Am I that affected already? A few months ago it would have been a fortune to me, an absolute godsend. Now it's just a bundle of notes I put in the bag to... to... to what? Cover the lads' petrol? Fuck's sake. What kind of a twat have I become?

"Well there's a fair bit more to come la so sit tight and I'll weigh you in when I get back. Nobody saw you then?"

"No mate, not a soul around, listen, five grand's fine for me la honestly"

"Don't be soft, just wait 'til I get back and we can talk properly yeah?"

"Sound fella, no problems. It's all safe anyway so enjoy the rest of your jollies"

"Will do kidder, will do"

"Ta ta" and the phone goes dead in my hand.

What a legend? What an absolute, bonifide, million percent legend?

I stroll into the shop with a smile on my face and a spring in my step but this proves to be short-lived as the newspaper headlines hit me like a shovel.

It's on the majority of front pages, staring up at me from the newspaper stand and I pick one up to examine it further.

LIVERPOOL TURF WAR!!! Is the headline, underneath which is a picture of what looks suspiciously like the burnt remnants of Rodney's house.

Apparently, the powers that be have linked Rodney to the others and are now of the opinion that there's a coup going on in Liverpool's fair city and the backlash has spread as far as Keswick. Apparently the execution of Lakeland dealer Rodney Parker (so that was his surname...) bears all the hallmarks of recent attacks in Liverpool and police suspect the same hitman off perpetrating the deed.

According to an unnamed source, there's a huge power struggle going on in the city at the moment, resulting in the deaths of some of the area's main players. So far no innocents have been caught in the crossfire but police believe that it's only a matter of time before this escalates out of control.

Detective Chief Superintendent Ralph Bailey said in his official statement that in his opinion, it's only a matter of time before revenge attacks rock the city and police and public alike must be on their guard at all times.

I pay for the paper and a carton of milk and saunter out of the door still reading these pearls of wisdom. If this truly is the case, then all eyes will be on the big hitters and far away from yours truly. This is actually fucking spot on, if I'm perfectly honest. What a smoke screen? What a wild goose chase? The city's bad boys and bizzies are going to be watching the higher echelons of the narcotics industry and won't even consider anyone as low key as Terry and myself. That's a thought. I wonder if he's heard anything?

I take the phone from my pocket, scroll to Terry's number and press the green button.

"Hello?" No familiarities, no friendly tone. Flat.

"Now then petal, how's it going?" I ask.

"Fine"

"Just fine?"

"Yeah la, just fine. What do you want?" he replies with a touch of petulance.

"Have you seen the papers?"

"Haven't I just? Fuckin' crackers isn't it?"

"Oh aye, good for us though"

"And how d'you work that out?"

"Well, all eyes are off've us now aren't they?"

"You reckon do you? One of JJ's lads has been round to see our Finchy"

This piece of information turns my stomach.

"What for?" I enquire, not entirely sure that I want to hear the answer.

"What d'you think?"

Fuck, fuck, fuck.

"Is he okay?"

"He's fine, didn't say a word. To be truthful he doesn't really know a lot to tell anyone does he?"

"Thank fuck for that" I sigh "D'you think they'll be paying me a visit?"

"Don't think so, our Finchy threw them off the scent for now"

"Nice one. Where are you?"

"Safe" is his curt reply.

"Safe?"

"Yeah la, safe"

"Like that then is it?"

"Yeah, it is and it's best if I don't know where you are either? Just in case like. I gather you've seen the pictures of Rodney's house?"

"Yeah" I reply, waiting for the accusation.

"Fuckin' right, somebody's on the rampage aren't they? And I'm fucked if I'm going to let them catch up with me"

Oh Terry, you little legend. A bit near sighted and isn't that just wonderful.

"I know what you mean. You're not going to be on the Oak on Sunday then?"

"Not fuckin' likely"

"What have you told H?"

"Just said I had family matters to take care of down in the smoke"

"And he was alright with that?" I ask.

"He had to be"

"Fair enough. Right then flower, I'll see you when I see you then"

"Not if I see you first" Terry replies light-heartedly but I can't help thinking there's an element of truth in the jest.

"Take it easy mate" and I press the red button.

What am I going to do now? I can't exactly move us all out of the house can I? But by the sound of what El Tel's just told me, things should be fine and dandy. No one's going to add this one up and come up with little old me are they? I'll just go back to work on the Oak and everything will be plain sailing. No danger.

God knows where Terry is and his absence might raise a few eyebrows, which is a worry. Don't think he should've been off on his toes so quickly but it's his choice at the end of the day.

No, I've just got to go back to my normal life, keep my head down and blend in. Should be easy enough. After all, I'm not public enemy number one now am I?

CHAPTER 47

THE REST OF THE HOLIDAY passes by in a blaze of sun filled days and beautiful, balmy nights.

My mind starts to settle down towards the last few days and I feel ready to face real life when we return home.

I've decided to just leave the bag full of money in the boot of the BM. Amy won't have any reason to look inside and I can take it out to the workshop when we get home. No problems. No dramas. Don't know what I was thinking at first. Panicking I suppose. The safest way to get the dough back to home base is to take it myself, obviously. Makes sense doesn't it?

I'm definitely going to have to get a bigger tool chest or something similar. There's no way this lot will fit in with the rest.

I never thought I'd see the day when I said this, but I'm starting to lose track of how much I've actually got. How fucked up is that? I've got a fortune at my fingertips and I don't know how much I've got and I know it's just through complacency. That's all it is. The five grand for Alfie was a classic example. How far removed from reality am I? Five thousand pounds is a lot of money. Only, not when you've got hundred's of thousands in your shed.

I should have the keys to the flat next week and the tenants will be ready to move in two weeks after that. How easy was that? The property will just sit there year in, year out, increasing in value, ticking over, looking after itself. Too easy.

The estate agent I got it from does a furnishing package for somewhere around two grand. They buy it all and move it in, which sounds absolutely ideal for my purposes and I've instructed them to go ahead as soon as I take possession.

I've arranged to see another apartment next week. A bit more grandiose this time though. A bit more up market. Nice two bedroom penthouse down by the dock. I'll have to put more money into the accounts, but judging from past experience, that shouldn't be a problem.

I know I'm going to have to tell Amy about all of this eventually, but I'm hoping that very soon, I can build our life up to such an extent that she'll believe I'm really earning Brewster's legitimately. Saying that, once the property game takes off properly, I will be.

It won't be long now before all this is behind me and I'm on an even keel. Just got to get through the next few weeks or months, however long it takes for all the nastiness to resolve itself. A few months from now I'll look back on all this and laugh.

CHAPTER 48

IT'S SUNDAY NIGHT AGAIN AND I'm standing on the door of the Oak with a new face for company. The lad's name is Glenn and he's from over the water somewhere. Not being rude, but this is all I want to know. I'm not going to be doing this for very much longer and the more I get to know about people, the more they will inevitably get to know about me and right now I want to keep as low a profile as possible.

He seems like a nice enough fella though and we pass the time discussing Liverpool's chances of ever winning the league again.

Terry's absence has been noted and enquired about but I've just been vague with the lad, saying that I haven't got a clue where he is, which isn't far from the truth.

As our discussion progresses, I watch the homeless and the druggies and the alkies stagger by in their quest for money to buy more of whatever it is that's put them in this horrible predicament. They're constantly swarming the city streets and it seems as though their numbers are increasing as the weeks wind on through spring and on towards summer.

Some of them just amble along, obviously in the grip of their preferred high, momentarily happy and at some sort of peace while the chemicals course through their bloodstream, firing receptors and inducing endorphins. Others pace by with that smackhead scuttle on an obvious quest to score. It's funny but they all have the same walk, like they're on a mission. They're faces fixed in determination as they soldier on down the street to their awaiting dealer to purchase a bag of indifference. Considering how much these apparitions eat, I'm amazed they have the strength to stand up never mind march across town like they do. I suppose addiction is like that though isn't it? If it's brought them this low there's no telling what it can get them to do.

Heroin. Considering the amount of publicity surrounding the drug and the stigma that goes with it, it never ceases to amaze me that anyone would actually try it in the first place. I mean, you never see a casual Heroin user do you? You never here anyone say 'Oh aye, I don't mind the odd jab of scag now and again' do you? It just doesn't happen. There are no casual users. From what I can gather you can become addicted within a week and then the rest of your life is just a living hell as you strive to find your next hit. Where's the fun in that? I really can't get my head round it at all. You'd have to have a death wish or something to even go near it. Fucking lunacy. All you have to do is look at these poor lost souls, damned to a lifetime of dependence and it'd put you off for life.

You may be wondering what happened to the bags of brown that we liberated from Jamie Buck's house and you'd be right to. Fact is, they're stashed in a very safe place. I haven't decided what to do with them yet. I don't know whether to try and punt them on or just get rid of them.

I'm not sure, but I think it's a similar price per kilo as the bugle, so there's a fair amount of money to be made from them. But do I really want to perpetuate the misery that I see trailing past me in this baghead parade?

I float back to the conversation and Glenn's deliberating whether Chelsea will be able to buy the league for the foreseeable future. Much as I dearly love Liverpool Football club, I just can't summon the gumption to get that involved in the discussion. My mind is awash with all of what's going on and I have to get out of it somehow. I don't want to be rude or appear above myself and in other circumstances I'd talk about the Reds until the cows come home, but this isn't the time.

"Fancy a Red Bull?" I ask him at a suitable gap in the conversation.

"Nice one" he replies and I trundle off up the steps to the bar.

The licensee, Napoleon, sees me coming and gets himself ready to tackle me.

As I approach the bar he pulls himself up to his full height, which is hardly worth the bother.

"Yes?" he enquires of me with a little more attitude than is necessary.

"Two Red Bulls please" I tell him.

"I've told you before Sammy, you can only have draught soft drinks for free, you'll have to pay for the Red Bull"

"What? Drink the bilge water that comes out of them pipes? Not fucking likely sunshine, just give us a couple a Red Bull and stop your whinging"

"But the brewery..."

"Fuck the brewery. Just pass them over. They're getting this door for a song anyway so don't be coming all that" I know this is a bit abrupt but I'm really not in the mood.

"They're not going to be happy" he says as he takes the cans out of the fridge and hands them across the bar to me.

"Not being funny lad, but do I really look like I give a shit?" Not like me. Not like me at all.

Napoleon is about to retaliate when several shots ring out from downstairs. I fly down to find Glenn lying twenty foot from the door on the concrete pavement, clutching at his profusely bleeding leg.

This is not good.

CHAPTER 49

THE AMBULANCE HAS TAKEN THE poor unfortunate Glenn away to the Royal and the CID have taken as many statements as they can, cordoned off the area and fucked off as well. Only forensics and a couple of uniform remain.

I'm stood here, shell shocked.

The big question is, what the fuck was all that about? Is this part of some door war? Did Glenn have any enemies or were they after yours truly? If they were after me, will they be going to my house right now? Slow down Sammy lad, slow down. If they were after you then they obviously think they've got you don't they? They won't be going to the house if they think they just gunned you down will they? Just calm down and think about it logically.

But what if they want to do a proper job? What if they want to annihilate you and all your family?

Fucking hell la this is Liverpool, not Sicily

Just as the quandary threatens to burst my weary brain, Big H pulls up in his Range Rover.

"You alright?" he asks as he slams his door and marches over.

"I'm fine, that Glenn took a couple in the leg though, poor fucker"

"Yeah I heard"

The pub has been able to remain open, as the crime scene is a way down the road. The poor twat must've seen the attackers and made a run for it before he was taken down by the flying lead. The forensic team are digging a few stray bullets out of the wall of the restaurant next door and by the looks of things a few of them were at head height. Lucky bastard.

"I'll stay on here with you 'til closing time" H tells me and I don't know if I'm reassured by this or not.

"Any idea what it was all about?" I venture.

H turns and looks deep into my eyes as if searching for something. I just return his gaze as best I can, trying my best to look innocent and unaware.

"I've got a few ideas la yeah" he replies still visually searching me "What about you?"

"Me?" I reply with as much incredulity as I can muster "I haven't got a Scooby mate, not my thing all this shit is it?"

"Isn't it?"

"Like I told you when I started H, I'm a family man, I'm not into all that gangster shit. I turn up on time, do my job, get paid, go home and that's it as far as I'm concerned. All of this call outs and drugs and all of that carry on is for other people"

I hope I haven't laboured the point here.

"Yeah I know that but what about Terry?"

"What about Terry?" I reply with a feigned look of incomprehension.

"He had a little somethin' going on didn't he?"

"How d'you mean?"

"Don't play the innocent with me, you know very well what I mean"

This really is shit or bust time and I'm struggling to think how I'd react if there truly was nothing going on. Would I deny all knowledge vehemently and retaliate verbally? Would this make me irate? Would I have an argument with the big fella right here on the door? Would I fuck, this is Henry fucking Haynes I'm talking to here.

"H, I don't know what you think is going on here, but I really have no idea what you're talking about"

"Everybody knows that you and Terry were thick as thieves and you can't deny it"

"Yeah we were… are good mates but if he's been up to something he hasn't said fuck all to me about it. I told him what I told you H, I want fuck all to do with anything illegal. I've got too much to lose haven't I? I'm tryin' to support my family, that's why I'm workin' on the doors and if I get nicked, not only will I lose my badge but my day job goes as well and that would just be plain disastrous. And I don't even want to contemplate what would happen if I were to get a stretch"

"Alright kidder, point taken. You haven't seen Terry lately then?"

"No, he's gone down south for a while hasn't he?"

"Yeah" H replies "Somethin' to do with family he said. You spoke to him on the phone?"

"Only briefly" I lie "He didn't really give any details"

"Alright. The next time you speak to him tell him to phone me. I've called him a couple of times but he doesn't answer"

"Will do"

I have to ask.

"So what d'you reckon's going on then?"

"People are getting twitchy with all of this recent caper going on. Nobody knows who's doing what and a few old scores will be settled amidst the confusion, know what I mean?"

"Not exactly, no"

"Old grudges can be settled under the cover of this recent spate of killings and everyone, including the bizzies will assume it's all to do with the same thing"

"Ah, I see. So what old score was this all about tonight then?"

"For someone who doesn't like getting involved you don't half ask a lot of questions" H says, looking straight at me again.

"I am involved though aren't I? If I hadn't've gone upstairs for a couple of drinks that could've been me couldn't it? Only I might not've been as lucky as that Glenn"

"Fair enough la, fair enough. Now you come to mention it though, it was a bit convenient you bein' upstairs and that wasn't it?"

"And what d'you mean by that?" I reply with a little more venom than I had intended.

"I'm just sayin' that's all"

"Sayin' what? I've never laid eyes on Glenn before tonight and you think I've had him shot? What the fuck's that all about?" I know this is big H, but I'm starting to get wound up now, starting to lose my rag with all this Q and A

"Fuckin' hell H, if you think this is down to me just come out and say it"

"Woe, woe, easy there..." H begins, but I'm away.

"Bollocks. I know you're the big fella and all, but I'm not gonna' stand here and take this off've anyone. In case you hadn't noticed I very nearly got shot here tonight. Standing on a door that *you* run. If anythin' I should be grillin' you 'cos let's be honest here, out of the two of us you're the most likely candidate to be the target for all of this shite aren't you?" I can see him tense up in retaliation mode but I'm too far gone "And if that's your attitude you can shove your door, I've had enough"

H moves towards me and I'm expecting a smack but instead his granite face splits in a grin.

"Alright la, alright, I know you've got fuck all to do with this but I've got to be sure haven't I?"

"Eh?" I utter in total disbelief.

"Listen lad, don't spew it, we need legitimate lads like you don't we?"

"Lads with badges you mean?" I reply, still partially vexed.

"Well yeah, that as well. Listen, you've done us a few favours in the past and we do appreciate that, so what I'm gonna' do is move you off've Vida's and onto O'Malley's for your Friday and Saturday nights. That'll be better for you won't it?"

O'Malley's is a busy little Irish bar, slap bang in the centre of town with no rats in hoodies or wannabe gangsters. This will do just fine.

"Yeah, it'd be a lot better than that fuckin' dump"

"That's sorted then. You don't want to be leavin' us now do you?"

"No H, I need the cash don't I?"

"Good lad, good lad. Is that Glenn's Red Bull?" he asks pointing to the can inside the foyer.

"Yeah" I reply.

"He won't be needin' it now will he?" and with that he cracks it open and guzzles the contents

"Now then" he continues "what do you reckon to the Red's chances of winnin' the league this season then?"

Fucking surreal.

CHAPTER 50

THREE DAYS HAVE PAST SINCE the shooting at the Oak and my nerves are starting to settle.

Perhaps the hail of bullets wasn't meant for me. Perhaps there's more going on in this beautifully corrupt city than all of my little shenanigans. Of course there is.

Word has it that that Glenn had a quite few interesting sidelines on the go, any one of which could have resulted in retribution of that nature.

It was touch and go at the hospital, according to H. One of the bullets had severed his femoral artery and they only caught it in time by the skin of their teeth. Lucky bastard. Saying that though, if some of the other rounds had of hit the target he would've been brown bread at the scene.

H keeps ringing me and asking me if I've spoken to Terry and I keep telling him that I haven't. That isn't exactly the truth of course, I spoke to him yesterday to inform him of the latest developments and of H's interest in his whereabouts and activities. Surprisingly he doesn't seem that bothered or concerned, he just said to tell H that I hadn't heard from him. Fair enough. I can do that.

It was Terry who told me about Glenn and his spirit of free enterprise. There's not many doormen in town that Terry doesn't know, or know about.

I'm sat here, in my office, staring blankly at the computer screen, trying to muster the enthusiasm to embark on the day's agenda when my mobile goes. I look at the screen to see that it's H again. I've never spoken to the man so much as I have done in the last few days.

I press the green button and put the phone to my ear.

"Hello H"

"Alright la, how's it going?"

"Not bad mate and you?"

"Boss la, Boss. How d'you fancy workin' on Bar Bella for us Tuesday and Wednesdays?"

"I'd rather gouge my liver out with a rusty spoon to be perfectly honest H"

Bar Bella is a moody gaff, full of wannabes and plazzy gangsters, all thinking they're the bollocks because that's where Tommy Monaghan and his boys used to drink before it all went tits up for them.

"I thought you needed the poke?" he ventures.

"Not that badly I don't"

"Come on la, we've only got three lads with badges on there and we need eight at least"

"Sorry H but I'm up to me eyes in it as it is, what with the day job and the kids and that, I just couldn't do it. Amy'd kill me if I took anymore nights on, she hardly sees me as it is"

"Alright la, alright. Can you just cover tonight for us though? I'll make it worth your while"

Fucking hell H I've got a shed full of cash in the back garden, how worthwhile is it going to be?

"I don't know H" I reply with a little less resistance than I had intended. Seeing a way in H ploughs on.

"Go on kidder, I'll give you sixty quid in your hand for five hours work"

A few months ago that would've been a nice little bonus, now it's fuck all. Sounds bad, but it really is fuck all. But I want to keep the big fella onside and keep up the pretence that I'm still on ordinary money. Can't go making out I'm brewstered just yet.

"What time from?" I enquire, knowing that I shouldn't.

"Only nine til' two, dead easy"

"Just for tonight though?"

"Just for tonight"

"Alright then" I reply with bitter resignation.

"Nice one la, I'll see you there later"

The phone goes dead in my hand and already I'm regretting what I've just agreed to.

CHAPTER 51

I ARRIVE AT TEN TO nine and a few of the lads are already there. I kind of know a couple of them but there's one I've never seen before sitting at the bar with a can of Red Bull in his hand and a scowl on his face.

Eddie Maddocks comes over and shakes my hand with his usual enthusiasm and enquires as to my well being. He absolutely loves all this Eddie does. Lives for it. He's a nice fella though and he's always pleased to see you. I worked with him on Vida's a couple of times and he's all day, bang up for it. Doesn't take any shit off've anyone, no matter who they are. He's a good lad to have on your side and I'm glad to see him if I'm honest. The lads work in twos here and I'm praying that I get paired up with him. I hope I don't get stuck with the moody twat at the bar, he looks like a right bundle of joy.

By nine bells all the lads are here and chatting away about which girl they've been banging this week and what depraved sexual acts they've subjected them to. I just stand on the periphery and take it all in. Some of the lads are quite funny. Eddie for example, can tell a story and have you in stitches, no matter what the subject. Should be on the stage that lad. Can hold an audience in the palm of his hand. Some of the other lads just come across as though they're braying. No sense of humour, no charm or wit, just bragging about what they clearly haven't done. Making up stories so as they can try to impress their peers in some sort of verbal battle for a place in the doorman's hierarchy. Laughable.

At a quarter past, H bounces in and enquires as to why there's no one on the door. We all file out, some with faces like naughty schoolboys, like they've just been reprimanded for talking in class.

Once outside, the banter continues, mostly directed towards H but he's not really interested in who's shagging who and after a few minutes he brings us all to order.

"Right then" he proclaims as he addresses the troops "We need four on the door tonight, I want a strong presence what with all that's been going on. Robbo and Macca, you take upstairs, Eddie, Marshy and Ben, you're out front with me and Sammy and Michael you're downstairs"

Bollocks! I've only got the moody twat haven't I? Fuckin' hell, as if this isn't going to be bad enough, I've got to put up with that miserable prick all night.

He saunters towards me but doesn't look me in the eye, just brushes past and makes his way downstairs. Fucking marvellous! This is going to be a long five hours this is.

I follow him down to an almost empty room to find him at the bar taking another Red Bull from the barmaid. The DJ's setting up to my left and the other barmaid is sitting at the end of the bar, but other than that the place is dead.

I walk over and ask the girl for a lemonade. Nice of my colleague to get me a drink in isn't it? Miserable cunt.

A couple of early punters stroll down the stairs with their best swagger. Sad, sad bastards, all dressed up like Fifty Scent with the jeans seven sizes too big, the basketball vest on over an equally oversized tee shirt and a bandanna on under their baseball caps. I wouldn't mind but they're white as a fucking sheet. You couldn't get whiter if you tried. I can just see the ginger hair of one of them poking out from under the bright red cloth of his headscarf. They're trying to talk the talk too. Putting on lisps with their pseudo-Jamaican accents and making wild exaggerated gestures with their hands as they talk loud enough so as I can hear them. Talking about weed and pills and weights. Fucking wankers.

I'll hasten to add at this juncture that I have nothing against the customs, fashions or people of any creed, culture or race, but when somebody tries to be something they're clearly not it fucking riles me. Especially when they're so deluded that they think they are in some way looking good with it.

If some of the lads from Granby come in here tonight and see these goons acting like this there'll be murder.

"You got any ID lads?" I ask them to their obvious surprise.

"Nah blood, don't need any" that accent again. Very fucking irritating.

"Says who?" I reply, my patience wearing paper thin.

"No one axthed uth on the way in"

"Well I'm *asking* you now"

"We don't got none"

"Well you're gonna' have to leave then" I tell them in my calmest tone possible.

"No way bro" the cockier of the two says "I'm out to 'ave a coupla' drinkth with ma thpar 'ere"

"Well you can have them some where else" I tell them as I place my hands on their backs and guide them towards the stairs.

"Get your handth off blood!" one says as he tries to move my hand off his back with his arm in a petulant gesture. That's enough for me and I slide my hands up their backs, around their necks and march them up the stairs in headlocks towards the front door. H sees me coming and comes in to grab one of them as he struggles wildly to be free. They're starting to panic now the pair of them, and surprise surprise their accents seem to have melted away.

"Fuck off will yer!" One barks at me from somewhere under my armpit. H grabs the other one and hurls him through the front door, onto the pavement.

"Who the fuck let them in?" I enquire when I've dispensed with my own captive.

"Why, what did they do?" Eddie asks.

"They didn't have ID for a start and they were actin' like a pair of pricks"

"Sorry la" Eddie says with a smile "Didn't even think to be honest"

I make my way back downstairs to see my colleague still sitting in the same place at the bar and it occurs to me, the cunt never even moved to give me a hand. Twat.

I walk over to him and pick up my lemonade.

"You can join in if you want you know" I tell him watching the blaze of hatred flash across his grid. What the fuck is his problem? He's not paid to sit at the bar looking moody is he?

The cunt just nods and takes another sip from his can. If he carries on like this I'm going to end up twatting him before the night's out, I really am. I need someone down here who's game and willing to get stuck in if needs be, not some morose arsehole with a chip on his shoulder the size of Seaforth. Why the fuck did I agree to this?

More punters start to filter in and, because of the size of the place, they make it look more empty. I hate this fucking dive, fucking despise it.

An hour goes by and still the miserable fucker has hardly said two words to me. I am never working here again, ever. My mind wanders to the bountiful box in my workshop and the delights therein which just makes this all the more ridiculous.

I'm about to go and check the toilets when my colleague leans over to me bringing his head close to my ear to be heard over the din of the music.

"You know Terry Quinn don't you?"

"Yeah" I answer, far from keen to engage in conversation with the lad now.

"You know where he is?" he asks.

"Haven't got a clue" I reply but before I've got all my words out he's on me, throwing wild punches.

"You fuckin' lyin' bastard!" he yells over the thump, thump of R and B.

I raise my guard to defend myself as the big mad haymakers bounce harmlessly off the sides of my head. I see a way in and take it. A straight shot right on the fucker's nose and he goes down like a sack of shit, blood and snot everywhere.

The crowd have cleared around us and the DJ is ironically calling out for security. Michael tries to get up to have another go but I'm not interested and floor him with a swift kick in the mouth. Cheeky twat, what the fuck was all that about?

H and Eddie come bounding down the stairs four at a time and race over to the little fracas. The look on H's face says it all and I prepare myself for another onslaught.

"Fuck's goin' on here?" he bellows at me, hand on my chest to prevent me inflicting anymore damage on the now profusely bleeding Michael.

"He just came at me H. Asked if I knew where Terry was and when I said I didn't he fuckin' flipped"

A look of recognition spreads across H's face and he hauls the bleeding mess to his feet and helps him towards the stairs.

"Eddie, stay down here' I'll send Ben down in a mo'. You come with me"

Back upstairs my ears are ringing as we stand in the foyer, not from the blows but from the deafening music. H bundles Michael into a taxi and tells the driver to take him to the Royal. Then he turns back to me. Before he's got a chance to say a word I take my chance.

"Honestly H, I haven't got a fucking clue what that was all about. The cunt never said fuck all to me all night, then he asks me about Terry, calls me a liar and fuckin' jumps on me like a man possessed!"

"You know who that is?" H asks me in a calm but calculated tone.

"Haven't got an earthly la" I reply in all honesty.

"That's Michael Carter. His sister died in the house fire with Jamie Buck"

The realisation hits me like a cannonball. I killed his sister.

"What's that got to do with Terry?" I enquire, trying to keep my face from betraying me.

H eyes me closely, examining every line on my face, searching for some clue or gesture that will signify my guilt or secret knowledge.

"Well" he begins "There's a few people of the opinion that Terry had somethin' to do with all that isn't there? Especially seein' as he's had it away on his toes so abruptly like"

"All what?" I ask as a delaying tactic. Got to get my shit together here. Got to make this a good one or I'm fucked.

"All of that caper with Jamie Buck and the three dealers that were ripped off on the same night"

"What, Terry?" I ask with as much incredulity as I can muster.

"Yes, Terry. We know he knew Jamie and we know he visited him not long before the fire"

Fucking hell, hark at Inspector Morse here.

"And what does that prove?" I enquire, my mind in overdrive in an attempt to conjure up an attitude befitting to the circumstances.

"Not a lot, but you know how people talk don't you?" H replies, still scanning me.

"Look, as far as I know, Terry is just an ordinary fella like myself, tryin' to scrape a living the best way he can. I can't see him killin' anyone can you?" I ask, turning the attention away from myself for a moment.

"You'd be surprised what money can do to people kidder, you really would. And anyway, Terry's not as clean cut as you're makin' out you know?"

"And how's that?" I reply, genuinely interested in what's coming next.

"He's been a bit of a bad lad in his time has our Terrance. Had his fair share of dodgy dealings if you get my drift?"

"No I don't H"

"He used to run gear around for Jamie Buck a few years ago. Made a tidy profit out of it as well by all accounts and word has it that he's disposed of a few unwanted obstacles for the Bucks over the years too"

"What kind of obstacles?" I'm not sure I want to know the answer to this question.

"People kind of obstacles la, you know what I mean"

I do now. You shady fucker Terry. You didn't inform me of this little piece of information did you? Fuckin' hypocrite, standing there, slating me for slotting Jamie Buck and that other wretch when all the time you'd been at it for years. Serial killers eh? I'll give you fucking serial killers you twat.

"Listen H, it's as simple as this; I haven't got a fuckin' clue what Terry's been up to right? I work with the lad and that's all. Whatever he gets up to in his own time is his business"

"Alright la, fair enough" H starts but I'm losing my rag.

"I've told you before H, if this is how it's gonna be; fuckin' Q and A every time I come to work then you can forget it. I've had enough. I haven't got a clue what he's been up to and I don't care to be perfectly honest and if that Michael wanker wants to start again I'll give him a proper goin' over as well, the cheeky twat, I'll break his fuckin' legs if he comes near me with that fuckin' scowl and attitude again no matter who's fuckin' died. D'you get me?" Too much Sammy lad, much too much.

"Alright la, calm down"

"Well, I'm pissed off with the lot of it. I only worked with Terry I don't live with the lad. Just let everyone know H, that I'm a separate entity to Terry right? Whatever he's been up to has fuck all to do with me"

"Alright la, fair enough" This seems to satisfy my inquisitive boss and he turns his attention back to the job in hand.

"Right then you can stay up here for the rest of the night, don't want you scarin' the punters downstairs do we?" Funny H, very fucking funny.

"Eddie can stay downstairs with Ben. Fancy a drink?"

Do I ever.

CHAPTER 52

GETTING UP FOR WORK IS always difficult when I've been on the door the night before. I've had four hour's sleep and my body aches from standing on hard concrete for too long.

I swing my legs out of bed and rest my elbows on my knees as I wait for the world to catch up.

It's seven o'clock. Amy and the kids are still asleep. The house is mine for the minute.

With a gargantuan effort I raise myself to my feet, don my dressing gown and make my way downstairs, feeling every step as my calf muscles sharply protest. I'm getting too old for all this.

It's only as I flick the kettle on that the girl's face swims into my thoughts. So that was her second name... Carter. Still can't remember her first name for the life of me. How bad is that?

I know the lad got on my nerves, but in all honesty he had every right to be fuming. If someone had killed my sister I'd be on the warpath as well. Ironically it turned out that he actually got his hands on the right fella too. Wonder how he'll feel about that if he ever finds out? He's not going to though is he?

It would appear that Terry is very much in the frame at the moment, and that concerns me. If they get to Terry then they get closer to me and I can't allow that to happen. As long as all eyes are off me, I'm happy for the moment, but if they ever do get a hold of Terry then things could come out. I'm not saying the lad's a grass or anything, far from it. No, what I mean is that he might crack under questioning, especially if the questioning involves torture, which it most probably will if stories about the Bucks are to be believed. Nasty bastards one and all.

This leaves me with a quandary and a loose end I could do without. As long as he's on the lam I'm fine. But then my safety depends on Terry's ability to stay hidden and his resolve to stay away from the North West and I'm not entirely convinced on either count.

I could really do with a good sit down with the lad. A good chat, one to one, to sort all this out so we know exactly where we stand. That would be ideal. Whether he would go for it is another matter. If I could find a reason that I had to see him, where there was no other way, then he'd have to agree to a meet. But what reason could be so important that he would give away his position to a potential enemy? That's what I am right now, a potential threat to his safety just as he is to mine.

I pour the boiling water into the cup and stir it's milky contents as the steam drifts up past my face. Think Sammy lad think. What possible reason could there be that he would see you?

"Morning Daddy!" I nearly leap out of my skin as my daughter's voice bellows from behind me.

"Morning sweetheart, how's my little princess today?" I ask her as I turn around and sweep her up in my arms.

"I'm fine" she says as she gives me a big kiss and a hug. "Can I make breakfast for Mummy?"

"Course you can darling, come on, I'll help you" and we both set about preparing a breakfast tray for my heavily pregnant, beautiful wife.

CHAPTER 53

ON MY WAY HOME FROM the office the A59's snagged up again. It's a bloody nightmare and a twenty minute journey takes almost an hour when it's like this.

I'd go the back way through Kirkby but it would probably take just as long.

So I'm sat here with the air conditioning on full. So much so that I'm starting to shiver ever so slightly. Can't stand the heat for too long. Makes me uncomfortable and irritable. Can't get my head round these people that lie out in the sun all day, baking like a scone. Not for me I'm afraid. I drive Amy mad when we're on holiday abroad. If I'm not in the shade reading a book, I'm off wandering somewhere, exploring and that. Can't keep still for too long even when I'm supposed to be relaxing. Just isn't me. Don't get me wrong, there are some times when I just need to unwind and relax for a while, but that only lasts for a couple of days at the most, then I'm up and off again. While her and the kids are by the pool, I'm off mooching around some local ancient ruins or strolling through a sixteenth century cathedral.

I must admit I've lit a candle or two in the past. Not that I'm a religious, but you never know do you? It always seems the thing to do in those places and I always get a feeling of awe in the presence of such amazing architecture. I know I'm rambling here, but I do. It never ceases to amaze me how these places could have been built so well with such basics tools and equipment, so long ago. They've been here for hundreds of years and will probably be here for hundreds more. It's a far cry from the prefabricated monstrosities that the Corpy threw up after the war.

But anyway, I digress. I've got a plan to get a face to face with El Tel. I'm pretty sure it'll work and I'm going to have to put phase one into action sometime next week. Shouldn't be too difficult, although it's going to involve a bit of graft initially, once that's over though, it's plain sailing from then on in.

It really was the obvious answer. Staring me right in the face all the time, in a manner of speaking. Guaranteed result this one. Just need to organise the equipment and location and I'm away.

I eventually get through Switch Island and the traffic thins out a bit.

At the traffic lights I look to my right at the Alt and next door at the supermarket where the Astra picture house used to be. I had some memories there, I can tell you and I was gutted when they pulled it down. It's funny how time runs away with you. One minute you're a spotty teenager, taking your judy to the flicks, the next you're married with kids, a mortgage and more responsibilities than you ever imagined possible. Crackers. Absolutely crackers.

I'm looking forward to getting home tonight though. Can't wait to see the beautiful faces of my adorable family. I can't believe how blessed I am to have such amazing people in my life. I'm sounding a bit soppy here I know but they're what gives me the strength and stamina to keep going in this bizarre world through which I stumble every day.

Will you have a listen to me? Don't know what's come over me today, but I'm feeling a bit needy. It's not an attractive characteristic really, but it's there all the same. I can't wait to feel Amy's arms around me and feel her lips kiss me. Can't wait to be in that house, safely locked away from the outside world. Just me and them and no one else. My family.

As I crest the canal bridge going into Maghull I realise that a tear is rolling down my face and I swiftly brush it away. What the fuck is going on with me today? Pull yourself together Sammy lad for fuck's sake, come on. This is not the way for someone in your position to behave.

I sail through Maghull and as the fields unfold on either side of me, I start to relax. I always do when I get to this point of the journey.

Around Robin's Island and turn right past where the Aughton Chase used to be. Past the waterworks on my right. The amount of times I've sat there fishing all day and caught fuck all but a cold you wouldn't believe.

Right at the Swan and up Smithy lane. This truly is god's country. It's beautiful.

Past the school that's now a rest home and up Bold Lane towards Town Green.

The Cockbeck (pronounced Coe-Beck for some reason that nobody really knows) sails by on my left and I'm over the bridge and turning right into Whalley Drive. Home, sweet Home.

As I approach the house I notice that the Golf isn't there and my heart sinks. She must be out. Shit. I really wanted her to be here. Bollocks. Now I'm pissed off. I wonder where she is? Must've taken the kids out or something.

I park the car on the drive and dejectedly trudge up the path to the front door. I put my key in the lock and as soon as the door opens, I'm instantly aware that all is not well.

There's an emptiness about the place and I can almost smell it.

In seconds I'm into the front room, back out and into the kitchen. Something's not right, I know it.

I race upstairs and into our bedroom and it's there that it hits me. Reality.

I fling open her wardrobe door and it's there for all to see. Empty. Not a stitch of clothing remains. What the fuck is going on here?

I fumble my phone from my pocket as quickly as I can and jab my thumb on speed dial 2.

It rings for what seems like an eternity until eventually I hear Amy's voice in a cautious "Hello?"

"Amy what's going on?" I ask, panic running through my voice.

"Oh Sammy, what have you done?" her voice tells me that she's close to tears.

"What d'you mean?" I reply racking my brain for an answer. What have I done? Well, if you've got a couple of hours…

"Someone came to the house today, said he represented a man called JJ, he said you'd know who he meant, his number's on the table" Shit, shit, shit…. "He said that some people want a word with you in connection with a shooting and that if you don't go and see them, we're all in trouble"

"Amy…"

"Don't Sammy, ok? Just don't. Frankly I would've just thought he'd got the wrong house and the wrong person if I hadn't seen that money in the boot on the way home from the lakes. There was thousands of pounds there Sammy, thousands and you're not telling me that you got that from the business deal are you?"

"No" I reply dejectedly. What else can I say?

"And you came back to the cabin smelling of a different washing powder, I mean, what was all that about? I turned a blind eye to it at the time. I didn't want anything to upset the wonderful time we've been having, but this? This is the top hat on all of it this is Sammy"

I don't know what to say. What can I say? I am guilty as charged. Bang to rights. Up to my neck in it.

"Amy I…"

"Don't Sammy, just don't. Answer me one question and I want the truth. What have you got us into?"

"Amy, we need to talk face to face, I can't do this over the phone"

"No Sammy. We're not coming anywhere near you, me or the kids. If you've been so reckless as to put us in this kind of danger then that's it. Just tell me that it's all a misunderstanding. If you can hold your head up and tell me that all the money is legit and above board and this horrible gangster is mistaken then we can work through this. But I want the truth. You owe me that at least"

What can I say? I can't lie anymore, not now. She deserves more than that. She deserves to know what kind of danger she is actually in and I need to tell her.

"I can't tell you that Amy, I don't want to lie anymore"

"Oh Sammy..." she wails and her every sob grates on me like fingernails on a blackboard.

"Amy please..."

"No Sammy, no. You've ruined it Sammy. You've ruined it all. I would rather have been poor for the rest of our lives than have a penny of this money, because that's where it's all come from Sammy hasn't it? All this extra cash we've had lately it's all dirty money isn't it?"

"Yes" is all I can say.

"So you have shot someone?" she tentatively asks, not wanting to hear the answer.

I can't lie

"Yes"

"I feel sick Sammy. Oh my god I feel sick to my stomach. How can you have done this? You're not a killer Sammy, you're Sammy, my Sammy. You're a father to my kids, you can't have killed someone" She's getting out of control now and I'm starting to panic.

"Amy calm down" but there is no calming her. Not now.

"No Sammy. You've ruined us. We're over. All this is over. You've destroyed everything"

"Amy no..."

"Goodbye Sammy" and the phone goes dead in my hand.

CHAPTER 54

I COME TO IN THE wreckage of our kitchen. There's broken crockery everywhere. The cupboard doors have been ripped off the hinges and the microwave's gone through the window. My own blood adorns the laminate floor and surfaces in wild swirling patterns and I can see that it's come from my weeping knuckles.

My head aches. The pain is so bad that it feels like my head will burst at any given moment. As I wipe my hands across my face I discover that my nose is bleeding as well. It's all down my chin and congealing on the front of my shirt.

The place looks like a bomb's hit it. Like Al Queda have been round for tea.

I've no idea how long it lasted or how long I've been sitting here in the middle of the floor in this chaos of my own creation, but I've certainly done a thorough job. The place is unrecognisable. Nice one Sammy lad, nice one.

The tears come flowing gently now and my body convulses with the effort to keep it all in. I'm terrified that if I give voice to my grief, I'll lose the plot for good.

I feel as though I've had my insides dredged out, as if I'm an empty shell. This is unimaginable. Unfathomable. Inconceivable. I can't have lost her, I just can't. She is the reason why I've done all this. Her and the kids. I only did it for them, so we could all have a better life. That was all.

Was it though? Was it really all for Amy and the kids or was there just a little bit of selfish intent there? Eh? Was there? I think there was, wasn't there? Just a little bit. Just a smidgen of me, me, me. You can't deny it. It's there for all to see. Written all over your face. You wanted the good life, the money, the car, the cash in your pocket didn't you? Didn't you? Of course you did. You wanted to be the boy didn't you? The man with the cash to flash and now it's all blown up in your face.

Shut up.

Why? Truth hurt does it?

Shut up.

Come on Sammy lad. You're gonna' have to face up to it kidder. You've thrown away the most valuable thing on this earth. The most precious thing on this or any other planet. Your family. Your *family*. Your pride and joy, your reason for living, your reason for existing, your life, your love, your family. Gone. All gone. For what? Money? Cash? Poke? Call it what you will, it's all the same at the end of the day. Folding stuff that means fuck all next to the loving warmth of your family and you just made the choice to put all that means anything to you in jeopardy for a few quid. That's all it was, a few measly quid. Fuck all in the scheme of things. Fuck all next to what you've lost and you have lost them Sammy lad, of that there is no doubt, There's no going back from here now.

Maybe I should have lied to Amy about killing someone?

What, more deceit? Come on now Sammy lad, don't you think we've had enough of that for one lifetime? After all it's deceit that's got you into this mess isn't it? Well isn't it?

Shut up

Why? I'm only speaking the truth aren't I? You know I'm speaking the truth. It would've been so easy to just've said no that night on the Oak wouldn't it? One simple word...no...dead easy isn't it? Dead fuckin' easy...no...N...O...No. Thankyou Terry but I'm not into all that. Family man me. Too easy. But you didn't did you? You wanted some of the spoils didn't you? Wanted the big money and if you're honest, you wanted to do it because you wanted to be the boy. Middle age crisis was it? Feeling like you're on your way to bein' over the hill? Bit of a dinosaur? Left behind by the ravages of time? You wanted it didn't you? Yes you fuckin' did and now it's too late. The die is cast, the dice are thrown, the cards are on the table and you're just going to have to play the hand you're dealt. It's as simple as that.

Shut up

Scary isn't it? To be on your own for the first time in years? Terrifying. Absolutely petrifying and to know you've put yourself in this predicament, well, makes it all the worse doesn't it?

Shut up!

Who are you talking to Sammy? Eh? There's no one here is there? Just you. On your own. Just you. Alone in an empty house. Just you.

CHAPTER 55

"WHAT THE FUCK'S GOIN' ON here la?"

I look up to see Alfie's face poking through the hole in the kitchen window, with a look of concern.

I've no idea how much time has elapsed. I've no idea what day it is if I'm perfectly honest. All I know is the feeling of desolation that fills my every cell.

"I've fucked up mate" I tell him "I've fucked up big time"

"Open the door la and let me in" he replies "Don't want to be discussin' this through a broken window do we?"

He's only right and I drag myself to my feet and crunch through the debris of broken glass and crockery, down the hall to the front door.

"Look at the state of your hands" he tells me as he closes the door behind him. I look at my knuckles to discover that they're swelling up to the size of boxing gloves. Blood stained boxing gloves at that.

We both sit down at the kitchen table and I hold my head in my swollen hands and I can't stop the tears from flowing. And they come with force. My body convulses with my sobs and at times I have trouble drawing breath. Alfie just sits opposite me. Waiting til I've finished.

Eventually the tears subside and I regain what's left of my composure. I look up into Alfie's face and proceed to tell him the story so far. He just sits there and listens, not saying a word, not even flinching, just listening. This is the first chance I've had, since coming back from the lakes, to speak to Alfie without Amy being present. I haven't even had chance to weigh him in with the rest of the dough yet.

When I've finished I look him straight in the eye and wait for a reaction.

"Well?" I say "What d'you reckon?"

"Fuckin' hell la, you don't do things by halves you do you?" he replies with a chuckle in his voice. I have told him everything by the way. Every little detail and to be truthful it's a relief to finally get it all out. To actually get it all off my chest in one go, the truth and nothing but the truth, feels wonderful.

"Where's Amy and the kids now then?" he asks.

"Probably at her mother's"

"Safe then?"

"Oh aye, safe as houses"

"Good, best place for them"

"How d'you mean?" I enquire, a little confused.

"Well, if this JJ fella's on the rampage, it's best that they're out of the way isn't it?"

"Yeah, course it is"

"Is right. Leaves us to deal with the rest of the situation with less to worry about doesn't it?"

"Us?"

"Yeah, us. You don't think I'm gonna' leave you to deal with all this on your Jack Jones do you?"

"But it's not your fight la is it?"

"Bollocks. I'll back you up all the way, you should know that by now"

"No mate, I don't want to drag you into all this shite as well. It's bad enough as it is without anything happening to your family"

"It won't though will it?"

"And how's that?" I enquire.

"No fucker's gonna' know anything about me or my involvement are they? We can do this nice and anonymous like"

"Do what?"

"Sort out the twat who left his calling card for a start"

"No, that's for me to deal with"

"But I…"

"Alfie lad, I appreciate your offer but it's my problem and I'm gonna' have to deal with it. It's good to know you've got my back if I need you though"

"Just say the word"

"I know la, I know. Here y'are, I haven't sorted you out yet for the other thing yet have I?" I tell him as I get up from the table and make my way to the back door.

"Don't worry about that mate" he says, but I'm adamant.

I lead the way out to the workshop and undo both locks. Inside I unlock the tool chest and start to count out five grand bundles onto the workbench.

"Fuckin' hell!" Alfie exclaims as his eyes feast on the sight before him.

"Crackers isn't it?" I grin.

"More than crackers la, it's obscene is what it is"

"There you go" I tell him as I hand him the cash "Fifty grand. Your share of the gear we got from the lakes"

"But I only picked it up"

"Doesn't matter, it's half yours and this is your cut"

He just stands there, mesmerised by the wedges of used notes sat in his hands.

"Sammy lad, what can I say?"

"Think nothing of it Alfred my old chum, think nothing of it"

CHAPTER 56

THE NAME ON THE PIECE of paper on the table was Anthony Jacobs, which led me to believe that he's a relative of JJ. Doesn't exactly take Sherlock Holmes to work that one out does it? A phone call to Terry confirmed it and he gave me a pretty good idea of where he lives.

I really must pay Anthony a visit. Think there's a few matters we need to discuss. Don't want to phone him though. Don't want him telling anybody else about our little rendezvous. That just wouldn't do. No, I think I'll pay him a surprise visit. I'm sure he'll be tickled pink at receiving an unexpected guest, especially considering he went to such lengths to get hold of myself, coming to my house, my family home. Doesn't get more thorough than that does it? He must really want a word with yours truly and I'm only too happy to oblige, only, on my terms and at my behest. That's the way it's going to go. At a time convenient to me. When I'm good and ready.

Standing here in my workshop, I'm turning over a cellophane package of brown powder in my hands. I've got a wonderful use for this little baby. Oh yes. This is fucking perfect. I knew it'd come in handy, just didn't realise it would be quite *this* handy. This package of filth is going to be instrumental in my safety and well being. It's funny how innocuous it looks. Just a package of dirty brown powder, not much bigger than a packet of sugar. Nothing special, nothing amazing, just a packet of shit. Horrible shit. Addictive shit. Shit that turns you into the person you never thought you'd be. Shit that ruins lives and families. Didn't need it to ruin my family though did I? Did that all by myself. No help from anyone or anything. All by myself. Me and my decisions. Just me.

CHAPTER 57

TERRY'S INFO WAS SPOT ON. Absolutely spot on. If there's one thing our Terrance knows, it's who's who in the narcotics trade in this fair city and the house wasn't that difficult to find from his directions.

I can see him through the window, pottering about in his kitchen, regular little Jamie Oliver this one.

Size of the house by the way. Fuckin' massive isn't in it. It's immense. Fuckin' immense. A bit more than his legitimate earnings could afford don't you think? Bit more than a dolite scumbag could reasonably buy on his meagre income. Despicable, if you ask me.

Look at him there, not a care in the world, sipping on glass of wine with a fuckin' apron on. Not very gangster that now is it? Not very Vito Corleone, an apron for fuck's sake. Just not cricket.

And here's me, camo'd up to fuck, squatting in the bushes of his rather extensive garden, peering in through his huge picture window while he prepares his tea. I'm just waiting to see how many plates he puts out before I go inside for our little 'tete a tete'. I need to know if he's got company. Damage limitation if you will.

There he goes out of the pan and onto the plate. Why Anthony, you flash twat, fancy going to all that trouble just for yourself? No companion tonight eh? No one to share your gourmet delights. Shame.

He leaves the kitchen and heads for the dining room table which, on closer inspection, is set for a cosy meal for one. Dear oh dear. Very sad. Looks like I'm gonna' have to go inside and keep the lad company.

This fella must really live in the glow of his family name. He must think he's untouchable. Leaving the back door unlocked Anthony? Big mistake.

And so, armed only with a claw hammer, I silently open the door and slip inside the kitchen. Taking care not to let my footsteps echo out off've the tiled floor, I ooze towards the door that connects to the dining room.

He's sitting there, with his back to me, blissfully unaware of his unanticipated houseguest.

I stand here for a minute, taking in the view of this man at peace in his own home. His sanctuary. His castle. Nothing but the sound of him masticating his feast fills the air and by the sounds of it he's certainly enjoying it. Bless.

"Not disturbing you am I?" I enquire as he jumps almost off his seat. Turning round, his face is a picture as he tries to work out who he's got in his house.

"What the f..." he begins as he makes an attempt to stand, but as he does, I bring the hammer round in a wide arc, ultimately connecting with the base of his spine. It has the desired effect. His arms flail out in a bizarre version of a star jump as he falls spread eagled on his expensive parquet floor. His screams are piercing as he desperately tries to claw himself along with only his arms for propulsion. His legs are gone, useless. The hammer has performed it's task admirably. He is paralysed from the waist down and completely at my mercy.

The noises coming out of his mouth sound almost inhuman as he squeals and wails in shear panic and distress and I can't deny, the sight of him in such a position is invigorating. I have no pity for this man whatsoever. Not a grain. This man has been to my house and now I'm in his. Only I don't like to leave things unresolved.

He looks pathetic, this so called hard man, this gangster, this bully. He is scrabbling at the floor, trying to find some purchase to grab and pull himself along, but his hands just glide over the polished surface making a squeaking noise with the slight friction. He is going nowhere.

"You don't mind me dropping by do you?" I ask "only, I get the impression that you wanted to see me quite urgently"

Incoherent babble is all I get in reply.

"I must say, it's a very nice place you've got here Anthony, very nice indeed. Must've been a bit pricey though, eh? Was it? I bet it was wasn't it? Very costly little pad this Anthony, but worth every penny I'll bet? Bit big for just yourself though don't you think? Bit greedy lad. But I suppose you'd have to be a bit greedy to get where you have in life wouldn't you? You don't get to be an important part of one of the city's top crime families by being happy with your lot now do you?

"I was happy with my lot Anthony, I really was. So happy you wouldn't believe. But all that's gone now, thanks to certain people. I've lost all of that, but we'll get to that later, right now it's all about you isn't it?"

I kick him onto his back so as I can look him in the eyes and the look of terror is priceless. I am relishing every second of this. He is helpless.

"You see the thing is" I continue "No matter how hard you are, no matter how revered you are, it only takes one person to change things for good for you. And I am going to change things for you Anthony, of that there is no doubt. You know that don't you? You know your life as a big man is over don't you? Don't you! Of course you do. That's why you're whinging like a baby isn't it? You're no fool are you? Course you aren't and you know you're life is very nearly over don't you?"

To this his wailing increases to a new and positively deafening pitch.

"Go on Anthony lad, scream all you want, no one's gonna hear you are they? That's the advantage of living out here in the sticks, away from prying eyes and ears isn't it? Scream all you want kidder, go on, fill your boots. In fact, I think I'll join you" and with that I let out the loudest, most hate filled scream I have and it feels good. More than good, it feels amazing and as I draw breath, I scream again and again and again. This just adds to poor, poor Anthony's terror and he goes into overdrive with his fruitless attempts to escape. No escape tonight though my poor, damaged, pitiful chum. No way. This is your last curtain call, your swan song.

I put my foot on his chest to steady him and look him square in the eyes again.

"You know you're going to die don't you? I mean, let's not beat around the bush here, you're on your last legs, pardon the pun, and it's up to you how you go. That is the only choice you have left in this life lad, d'you get me? The only thing you have control over is the manner of your death. Would you like to hear your options? Would you? I know I would. Got to be able to make an informed decision now haven't you? That's only fair. Only right.

"On the one hand, you could tell me what I want to know and I'll make it quick and relatively painless; short, sharp blow to the back of the head. Instant blackout. Goodnight Vienna. Nice and weighty this old hammer I'm sure you'll agree" I tell him as I let the hammerhead fall into the palm of my hand time and time again to illustrate the efficiency of my weapon of choice.

His eyes open wider than I have ever seen anyone's open before. They look like huge pink pinballs almost bursting out of their sockets.

"Or, and this is the big one, if you don't sing like the proverbial canary, I'm gonna' smash each one of your fingers individually and work upwards from there until every bone in your body is pulverised. Then, when you think it can't get any worse, I'm gonna heat up one of your beautiful silver knives over there, 'til it's glowing and I'm gonna' pop those fuckin' huge minces of yours, am I makin' any sense?"

"YESSS!" he screams. Think I've got my point across, what d'you reckon?

"Good lad Anthony, good lad. So what's it gonna' be? Eh? How d'you want it? Easy way or the hard way, it's up to you. I really don't mind either way. You see you've been instrumental in me losing everything I ever cared about, did you know that? Yes you have. So I really have abso-fucking-lutely nothing to lose and to be perfectly honest, I really want to make someone suffer for my loss, d'you understand me? Granted it was partly my fault for getting into all this shit in the first place but that's not the issue right now is it? No it isn't matey, it's all about you. You, you, you, you, you. Anthony Jacobs, man amongst men. Big man. Hard man. Dead man"

I'm starting to lose him now. The far away look in his eyes tells me his mind is shutting down to spare him the pain and emotional torment, but I'm not about to let him off the hook that easy. A swift slap around the chops brings him back to reality central and I fix him with my gaze.

"What's it to be then? Choose now or I'll make the choice for you and you might not be entirely happy with my selection"

"I'll tell you anything you want to know, anything!" he blurts.

"Good lad, I knew you'd be sensible about it. No sense in making things worse for yourself now is there? No point in being the martyr is there? Course there isn't. You know it makes sense. Now, if you tell me any lies or mislead me in any way, you're beautiful daughter is gonna' find out what the business end of a claw hammer feels like do you get my drift?"

Terry is a wonderful source of information.

The look in Anthony's eyes says it all. He knows I know.

"That's right kidder. Twenty seven New Lane, Aughton, Lancs, L39 4UD. Am I right?"

He doesn't have to reply. It's written all over his face. Plain as day. Got him.

"Good lad. It's best that we're both singin' from the same hymn sheet isn't it? Course it is"

Anthony nods enthusiastically like a kid that's been asked if he wants ice cream.

"I knew you'd see things my way" I tell him with a grin "Do you actually know who I am?"

"S...S...Sammy Jackson?" he stutters.

"That's right kidder, Sammy Jackson. Say it again"

"Eh?"

"Say my name again, go on"

"S...Sammy Jackson"

"Good lad. And again"

"Sammy Jackson"

"Well done la. Top marks. Sammy Jackson, that's me. Not a name you'll of heard of before though is it? No it's not. I am not a name. I am not a face. I am not known in this city as someone to look out for am I? Well am I? It's alright la, you can answer"

"No" comes his feeble reply.

"No I'm not, but you are though aren't you? Anthony Jacobs. Strikes fear into the hearts of men that name doesn't it? Anthony Jacobs. Don't fuck about with him la, fuckin' psycho. He's the fuckin' boy old AJ isn't he? Not to be trifled with. Not to be messed with, but I'm messin' with you now aren't I? Fuckin' right I am and who am I? Fuckin' no one that's who. Nobody. But this nobody is gonna' bring about your untimely demise mate. Nothing surer. I am gonna' end your life in a few minutes from now and there's fuck all you can do to stop me is there? There's no one who can help you, not out here. Not now, so you re fucked. Doesn't matter what your name is now does it? Doesn't matter if you're Al fuckin' Capone now does it? You are dead. Plain and simple"

The tears are coursing down his face now and I could almost pity him, but I won't.

"Come on now la, there's no need for all that is there? Surely you didn't think you were just gonna' ramble on into old age did you? What's the saying? Live by the sword, die by the sword? Well this old hammer isn't exactly a sword but I'm sure it'll suffice"

Sobs now. Big accentuated sobs. Crying like the proverbial baby. He knows it's all over and he's regretting now. Regretting ever getting into this line of work. Regretting ever having seen a class A. A job at the factory and a working class wage looks like heaven to the lad right now. No going back though. Not now.

"Right then kidder, it's show time. Remember, you're playing for the star prize, which is the life of your daughter so careful with those answers. Okay. The impending death you've already won is safe. That's going nowhere and the burning of your body and all the evidence thereafter, that's safe too. What you've got to weigh up is do you want to gamble? What do the audience reckon? What? What's that? I think they want you to play it safe Anthony what do you reckon?"

"Okay! Okay!" he blurts out.

"Good lad. Right then. I want you to give me the addresses of all of your storage facilities in relation to the naughty stuff, then I want you to give me the addresses of the rest of your brothers and an overview of their movements and you'd better be spot on with these kidder, cos' see if anything happens to me, there's someone out there with instructions to visit your daughter and give her a little reconstructive surgery if you get my meaning?"

He just nods his head vigorously again as I pull my notebook and pen out of my rucksack, sit on one of his beautifully ornate dining room chairs, cross my legs, pen in hand and give him my best quizzical look.

"Right then kidder, when you're ready"

Chapter 58

I'VE OFTEN WONDERED WHAT IT takes to make someone a man to be revered, to make him a name or a face. Obviously a propensity for violence is a significant part of it, that goes without saying. But there's a considerable amount of lads in this fair city who can have a fight and who aren't regarded in the same vein as this fella before me. What gives him that little bit extra? What is it that makes him that cut above the rest of the mushers and the bruisers? Is it guile? Is it intelligence? Is it Charisma? Fucked if I know and looking at this snivelling wretch on the floor here, it's hard to see anything that stands out from the norm.

"Now are you sure that's all completely kosher? There's nothin' you've left out or forgotten to tell me?"

"No, that's the lot, I'm tellin' you"

"Oh you're tellin' me are you? That's very kind of you la, you're tellin' me? Well you better be tellin' me right cos' you know what'll happen if you're not don't you?"

"Yes" he replies with a certain amount of resignation in his voice.

"Good stuff. Right, what have you got for me here?"

"Eh?"

"Come on kidder, don't be shy. You must have somethin' lyin' around here somewhere mustn't you? Tell you what, either you tell me now, or I'll go hunting and if I find anythin' you haven't told me about, it's torture time for your good self, am I makin' myself clear?"

"It's in the cupboard under the stairs"

"How original?"

I nip through to the hall, open the door under the stairs and sure enough, behind a few coats and shoes, is a large sports bag with a plethora of goodies inside. Bingo! Thankyou very much Mr Jacobs, most kind.

I stroll back to the dining room in time to see my victim reaching for the door of his sideboard, a look of desperation on his twisted face.

"Can I help?" I ask as I spring across the room and open the cupboard door before he has chance.

"Well, well" I sigh "This really is too kind of you Anthony, too kind"

At the back of the shelf, sitting there plain as day, is a snub nosed revolver.

"Was this what you were after?" I enquire as I feel it's weight in my hand. His face is a picture now. Terror isn't in it. Absolutely mortified he is. This was his last chance, his one hope of survival.

"You weren't thinkin' of shootin' little old me were you big fella?"

No reply. He can't reply.

"That's not very hospitable that now is it? Not a polite way to treat your guest"

He just crumples up into a heap. I think he's had enough now and to prolong it anymore would just be sick. I've made the twat pay and now it's time I put him out of his misery. Only fair isn't it? After all, I'm not a monster am I?

"Come on then Anthony lad, let's get this over with eh?"

His reaction is rapid. He's knows this is it and every survival instinct in his body is screaming at him to do something. His whole upper body tenses as he prepares for the end.

"Let's turn you over on your front eh? Be a lot easier that way. I can get a better swing then, cos' we don't want to have to do it in two now do we? That wouldn't be nice would it? Not very nice at all, no, I want to do it in one, nice and clean like"

He's convulsing with panic now as I roll him over to expose the back of his skull. As I do, his hands instinctively come up to cover his head.

"Don't be doin' that la. That's not gonna' work is it? Don't be daft. I'll only break your fingers and then I'll have to take a second swing and that's gonna' hurt isn't it? Of course it is, now move your hands or I'll move them for you"

Slowly, he draws his hands away and places them, palms down, on the floor.

"That's it, well done. Okay on three yeah?"

He's tensed tighter than a violin string and you can see the sinews sticking out of the back of his neck.

"One…" I bring the hammer down in a huge arc to meet the base of his skull and the sound it makes on contact tells me I've hit the target. Well, I wasn't going to make him wait til' three now was I? That would've been fucking cruel that would.

I take off my latex glove to check his pulse but I can see by the vacant stare that life has been extinguished. A job well done even if I do say so myself and surprise, surprise there's no feelings of nausea. The contents of my stomach are well and truly fixed in place.

I remove the canister from my rucksack and liberally distribute the petrol around the palatial surroundings. This is getting to be a habit.

Chapter 59

THE REVOLVER THAT I ACQUIRED from Mr Jacobs's house will come in more than handy, I'm sure, as this is far from over. I don't know if anyone will connect myself with his demise but I'm not taking any chances.

I've cancelled the tenants for the apartment in Cheapside and moved in myself. It would be shear lunacy to stay put at the house in Aughton in the current climate. There may be no retaliation, but to just sit there and wait would be foolish. Nobody knows about the nice little studio with a view of the Liver Birds from the balcony and that's the way it's going to stay. It's already been furnished by the estate agent so it's just a case of taking my clobber, my wedge and the stash of class A's that I'm steadily accumulating. I really am going to have to find a buyer for all this. There must be half a mil's worth here at least, what with the beak from Rodney's and the brown from Jamie Buck's and I need to convert it into hard cash as soon as.

The list I got from Mr Jacobs seems pretty comprehensive and I'll have to make haste if I'm going to get round to seeing all the names on it.

I still haven't spoke to Amy or the kids and it's killing me. The baby's due any time now and the feelings of guilt and loss are crushing. I don't even know if she's going to allow me to be at the birth and to miss out on such a miracle doesn't bear thinking about. I hope she's ok, her and the kids. Can't believe how much I miss her. It's like my guts have been scraped out and there's just a void inside me. A massive, gaping void. This is torture. This is pure, unadulterated, torture and I don't know if I can stand much more of it. My head feels like it's been in a blender.

I thought I might feel a little better after exacting my revenge on the poor unsuspecting Mr Jacobs, but it hasn't even made a dent. I feel wretched. Remorse is always the worst feeling as it's something you can't do a thing about. You just have to ride it, but the fact of the matter is, I don't know if I can. It's just too painful. If I'm destined never to see them again I can't see the point. What kind of life can I lead without them? All the cash in the world couldn't make up for what I'm losing and the thought that it's the lust for money that got me into this mess makes me sick to my stomach.

If I could just talk to her, just for a minute. Just to hear her voice and know that she's ok. But she won't answer her phone. I've spoke to her dad and he reassures me that her and the kids are fine, but that's not enough. It's just not. He's been ok with me and I know he won't have a clue as to what's gone on. There's no way Amy will have told him anything like the truth. He'd be straight down to the bizzy station, no danger, if he got wind of all that I've been up to. Of that there is no doubt. Straight laced the old fella is. Pillar of the community. Some of his best friends are on the force so it wouldn't be difficult for him. No, he just thinks we've fallen out and he actually wants us to get back together, bless his cotton socks. Funnily enough, they think the sun shines out of my arse, her mum and dad, always have done. Don't think they'd be so approving if they knew the full story though. Not what you'd expect from a son-in-law is it? Drugs and murder? Not very PC that now is it? Not something to brag about down at the golf club.

Got to do something. Can't just sit here and let all this happen. Got to find a way to talk to her, if only for a minute. Can't believe what I've thrown away. How could I have been so oblivious to the possible, no probable consequences of what I did? Thinking back now, it riles me how flippantly I agreed to be part of this charade. It took a second, that's all, just a second to dive in with both feet. No deliberation, no consideration, just a firm yes I'll have some of that. Money, money, money. Greed and gluttony, pure and simple. What a twat? What an absolute, hundred percent twat? You could say I deserve what I've got and maybe you'd be right. Maybe I'm not worth their love and respect? Maybe I never have been? Maybe it's taken this to illustrate that I'm way bellow their standard and not worthy of their time?

Pull yourself together Sammy lad, for fuck's sake! You sound like some old tart snivellin' on there kid. Just get a grip lad. You did it for them didn't you? Well didn't you? Of course you did. Fuckin' hell la you were goin' under at the time weren't you? Financial disaster would best describe it and you did what you thought best at the time for your family didn't you?

It hasn't worked out for the best though has it?

Says who? Amy'll come round la, she always does.

Not after this.

After what? So you've robbed a few scumbags, so fuckin' what?

And killed them.

But they were only scumbags weren't they? The shite on your shoe, you didn't kill any real people did you? Did you fuck! Just horrible twats who deserved much worse. You've rid society of some of the worst parasites haven't you?

Amy doesn't see it like that though.

She will la, she will. Just keep your chin up and ride the storm and let's have no more of that defeatist talk okay? It's makin' me sick listenin' to you drivel on. You need a bit of backbone at a time like this, bit of mettle, not fuckin' remorse and regret, they'll get you nowhere kidder, trust me.

Chapter 60

D'you know what? I fuckin' hate drunk people. Fuckin' despise them. Standing here, watching them fall in and out of the Oak, absolutely twisted on a Sunday night makes me cringe. The shite that some of them come out with as well. Fuckin' priceless. Mindless bollocks and the daft thing is, they really think you're interested in what they're telling you as they stand there, invading your personal space and blathering on, completely oblivious to the spittle shower that cascades from their rancid mouths. Even when you push them away they don't get the message, just carry on regardless like I give a shit.

This one here is really starting to wind me up and I can feel my fist clench instinctively. I've pushed him away to arms length but he's still intent on telling me all about his bird and how she's gone off in a huff cos' he was talking to some other girl at the bar and do I really care? This conversation needs cutting short as I've just seen someone I really need to speak to.

I turn my attention back to the mouth on legs next to me.

"Listen mate, I really couldn't give a toss about you or your bird, so do me a favour and fuck off will you?"

He looks at me with an expression nothing short of hurt.

"Fuckin' hell mate there's no need to be like that is there?" he exclaims "I was only sayin'…"

"Yeah well go and say somewhere else lad, you're givin' me a headache"

"Fuckin' bouncers" he mumbles to himself as he wanders off up the road at a stagger.

"Badger!" I call out as my mark is about to turn the corner into the next street. He turns with an instinctive flinch.

"Over here" I tell him and he dutifully ambles over, clad as ever in the same stinking, filthy garb. Toes poking through the end of his trainers, stains from several decades adorning his entire ensemble. The engrained dirt on this fucker's hands looks like it's been there since the dawn of time. Oh sweet heroin, you are a costly lover.

"Alright Sammy lad" he rasps as he approaches, shoulders hunched, head hung over, looking up through the mass of dirty black hair that seems to engulf his entire head.

"How's it goin' kidder?" I enquire, not really interested in the answer.

"Not too bad Sammy, I've got a phone for sale if you're interested" he suggests as he pulls a tiny flip Samsung from the recesses of his disgusting jacket and displays it to me in a conspiratorial manner, turning his head from side to side on the lookout, not for police, but for other bagheads who will steal it off him at any given chance. He'll have found it on the floor after some pissed up reveller has dropped it and not even realised. You'd be amazed at the amount of phones that end up this way.

"Not my thing Badger, you know that lad"

"Worth a try though eh?" he says as he quickly secretes his booty deep within the labyrinth that is his clothing. It never ceases to amaze me how many layers of clothes these people wear, even in the height of summer.

"I've got a bit of a proposition for you if you're interested" I tell him and his eyes light up with a blend of caution and intrigue. A baghead will do anything for money, absolutely anything, they'd sell their own mother for a bag of the other.

"Go on" he gestures, hopping from one foot to another.

"What I want you to do fella, is go and have a party with this little chunk here" and with that, I casually hand him a small, clear cellophane bag, containing a familiar looking brown powder.

His eyes light up, I mean literally. You could go potholing with them minces of his, positively beaming they are. He takes it from me with just short of a snatch then quickly looks up to check my reaction.

"It's alright Badger lad, it's yours to do with what you want"

"Fuckin' hell Sammy, there must be an eighth here easy!" He exclaims as he lovingly turns the packet over in his hands. Then, as if remembering where he is he rapidly deposits the package in the same direction that the phone went.

"What d'you want for it?" he asks me cautiously as he eyes me up and down. His face telling me that he's done some pretty awful things in the past for a lot less.

"Don't worry lad" I tell him with a smile "It's not your body I'm after"

He visibly sags as he realises his arse is safe.

"No, what I want you to do is go away to wherever it is you go and try this tackle out, but be very careful, its fuckin' rocket fuel this stuff, very pure so go easy on it yeah?"

"Yeah" he replies with a smile that shines out from underneath his forest of facial hair.

"And if you're happy there's a lot more where that came from. All I need from you is a little favour and I'll give you enough of that filthy shit to keep you pinned til' Christmas, that sound good to you?"

"Fuckin' is right Sammy lad, is right"

"Now don't go makin' a pig of yourself will you"

"No Sam, I'll take it easy I swear"

"Good, you're no use to me on the mortuary slab now are you?"

"No Sammy. What's the favour?"

"All in good time Badger lad, all in good time"

CHAPTER 61

I'VE JUST HAD A CALL from her dad. She's had the baby. A little girl. Eight pounds, eleven ounces. Mother and baby are both doing fine.

I am gutted. Unbelievably gutted. I've missed out on the birth of my child and the feelings of loss and desolation are killing me.

This is not fair. This can't be happening. I'm having trouble thinking. My mind is swamped in a deluge of despair. I am nothing. I am scum.

I am mentally dead.

Someone is going to pay for this tonight. Someone is going to pay with their life.

CHAPTER 62

ANTHONY'S LIST IS PROVING INVALUABLE and above all, correct.

This one was a bit of a struggle and unfortunately I've had to plug his Mrs as well but hey, that's the way life goes. Mouthy cow she was an' all. Proper foul mouthed, guttersnipe right up until the end. She's not gobbin' off now though is she? Fuckin' moose.

The haul from this gaff hasn't been quite as lucrative as the little lot I liberated from Anthony's, but it's been well worthwhile. Got myself another nice little shooter for use at a later date and a few grand. No gear though, which in some way is a relief. I still haven't got shut of all the other stuff yet and finding a buyer to take that amount off my hands in one go is proving difficult to say the least.

I take one last look around the house of Mark Jacobs and the opulence he has until very recently enjoyed, then I look down at his blood stained corpse. What a fuckin' waste? What a fuckin' joke? Mark Jacobs? Who the fuck are you now, eh? Who the fuck are you? No one that's who. Big, fat nobody, that's who. Laughable.

Oh well, out with the petrol and on with the gas oven. Same aul routine, different house.

189

CHAPTER 63

IT WAS VERY NICE OF Terry to give me Finchy's number, very nice indeed. I've set up a meet for next Tuesday and all the groundwork is set. Everything is falling into place. The lad thinks I'm meeting him with a view to a drug deal and in a way he's right. Just hope he doesn't get in contact with El Tel in the meantime. I've tried ringing Terry myself for quite a few days now and his phone is always off so I doubt whether Dopey has been able to get in touch. Marvellous. Absolutely fucking marvellous.

Stood here, on the Oak again, I'm starting to see a bright side to all this mayhem and chaos. All the loose ends are coming together to be tied up once and for all. If all goes according to plan I should be well in the clear before long and that suits me just fine.

I've been doing the Sundays here on my own since the unfortunate Glenn took a couple in the leg and that's been a godsend as well. It's given me the scope to put certain parts of my master plan into operation and here comes a large part of that plan now.

The reason why I picked Badger for this little task is that I know for a fact that he's ex-military. Irish Guards I'm told. Decorated for gallantry in battle and all that carry on. The sad fact is that Gulf War Syndrome has took it's toll on the poor lad and reduced him to the shambling wreck that I see shuffling up the street towards me now. I suppose heroin's cosy numbness would seem preferable to going through the horrors that GWS leaves you with. Poor fucker.

It's disgraceful that this is how we treat our war heroes. This man has fought for our country and we've left him out to dry.

"Now then Sammy lad" he gleefully greets me as he sidles up to me in a manner most shifty.

"Badger" I reply "How's tricks?"

"Fuckin' spot on Sammy lad, spot on. That tackle was A1 kidder, fuckin' sweet as fuck. Where did you get it from?" he enquires with a look of hope on his otherwise downtrodden face.

"A friend"

"You said you could get some more didn't you?"

"All in good time Badger lad, all in good time. You'd like a bit more of that though wouldn't you?"

"Oh aye Sammy lad, that was fuckin' amazin' stuff that was. Top notch"

"So you're prepared to do a little favour for me then?"

"Fuckin' right mate, just name it" he replies, desperation running thick through his voice.

He really would do just about anything right now to get his hands on some more of that lovely gack. Right now, at this moment in time, all he is concerned about is getting some of that filthy brown poison into his decaying, collapsing veins. Nothing else. Pure and simple. His body will be screaming for it. Begging for it. Pleading for it. The stomach cramps and shivers will be almost unbearable and to take all this agony and anguish away is his only concern.

"Follow me" I tell him as I lead him round the side of the Oak, down the dimly lit back street to my awaiting car.

As I reach the boot I turn and look him straight in the eye.

"Now can I trust you Badger?" I enquire of this virtual Zombie stood before me.

"Of course you can Sammy, of course you can"

"Are you sure?"

"Dead sure mate. Honestly, I won't let you down"

"Cos' once I open this boot there's no goin' back now, you do understand that don't you lad?"

"Yeah Sammy, yeah. Whatever you say"

He'd agree that the moon was made of cream cheese right now if I told him so.

"And you're happy to go along with whatever it is I require of you?"

"Yeah Sammy, of course, anything, absolutely anything"

I'm toying with the lad now and it's getting a bit sick.

"Okay" I tell him as I open the boot to reveal a kilo bag of brown and the shooter I acquired from Mark Jacobs's house.

"What the fuck?" Badger stutters as his eyes take in the glory of the sight before him. I don't even think he's registered the gun, he's that fixed on the bag of smack. Mesmerised isn't in it.

"What d'you reckon then? Like to get your grubby little mitts on that lot would you?"

"Not 'arf Sammy lad, fuckin' hell, it's beautiful" he drools. Got him. Hook, line, sinker and fishing basket. This is a done deal.

"You see the piece next to it?" I ask him.

"Yeah" he replies, still in potential opiate heaven.

"Well that's gonna' be part of the favour you're gonna' have to do for me in order for you to get your hands on that pretty little parcel there, d'you get me?"

He turns to me and for the first time his face shows realisation.

"Who d'you want me to slot?" he asks casually as if he was asking how many sugars I have in my brew.

"Billy Buck"

Silence. Long, slow, deafening silence until eventually he finds his voice.

"Fuckin' hell Sammy lad. Billy Buck? You're jokin' aren't you?"

"Not at all Badger, not at all. I want you to shoot Billy Buck in the head as many times as you can and if you can do that, the parcel's yours. Dead fuckin' easy"

"But..."

"But what? He's fuckin' human, same as the rest of us isn't he? He's not fuckin' immortal is he? He'll bleed just like the rest of us and he'll die the same as the rest of us won't he?"

"But how the fuck am I gonna' get to him?" he asks nervously as he can see the possibility of this big bag of heaven slipping through his fingers.

"Don't you be worryin' about that la, I know just the right time and place, that's not the problem. The big question is can you do it?"

The bag of scag is far too enticing and his urges and needs make the decision for him.

"Fuckin' dead right la"

"Good lad. I knew you'd see it my way. Now here's a little bit just to take the edge off" I tell him as I hand him a small bag I've pulled from my pocket. "Don't want you rattlin' when you're tryin' to take your shot now do we? But I don't want you getting' that twisted up that you can't do the job neither"

"No, I won't let you down Sammy lad, honest"

"You better hadn't, cos' there's a lot more than just a key of smack ridin' on this if you get my meanin'?"

"I know Sammy, don't worry, I won't let you down. You know me"

Do I fuck.

CHAPTER 64

SITTING HERE, WAITING FOR THE lad to turn up, I watch the constant flow of people going about their everyday business and I can't help but feel jealous at the apparent blandness off their lives. These people, office workers and the like, buzzing around like insects, shuffling from A to B, the worst fear they have is not being able to pay their bills, or if they're going to be able to afford a holiday this year. I wish my life was that simple. It used to be that simple before all this nonsense started. They say the grass is always greener and that maybe so, but the grass is tainted with pesticide and pollution on the side I currently stand.

I take a long sip of my coffee and shiver as it's warmth hits my stomach. It's not that it's cold outside, far from it, it's just that someone has just walked over my grave. It's always been a saying that's intrigued me that one; someone's just walked over my grave. Does that imply that I'm already dead and don't realise it yet? Does it mean that someone has walked across my burial plot in the future? I mean, what the fuck is all that about? Whatever it is, it's unnerved me. This is a public place and there are a lot of potential witnesses about.

Maybe meeting him in a crowded place wasn't such a good idea? Would he have agreed to a meet in somewhere more private and secluded? Probably not. I know I fucking wouldn't in the current climate. Things are very shaky in the Liverpool underworld at the moment and nobody has a clue who's doing what. Little do they know eh? Who would guess that little old me was causing all this confusion and mayhem?

The press have blown it up out of all proportion as you would expect. Headlines like LIVERPOOL AT WAR! And GANG-LAND OUT OF CONTROL, have been strewn across every major newspaper in the country. Granada reports are constantly giving updates on the situation and local residents groups are up in arms about the dangers to their children. There is no danger to their children though is there? Not unless they're related to the Bucks or the Jacobs's and only then if they're directly involved in the day to day running of their criminal empire.

The police and criminal fraternity alike are stumped as to the identity of the perpetrator or perpetrators and the fingers of blame have been pointing in all directions. Not at yours truly though. No one's going to put this down to me. The more it escalates, the further I drift out of contention and that's just fine for myself.

Big H has stopped questioning me about Terry and all that too. I barely get a grunt from him now when I go in to get my wages and that's fine as well. I've fallen back into the rank and file as far as Mr Haynes is concerned and I'm tickled pink with that. I'm just Sammy Jackson, family man again. Good old Sammy, always on time, never takes a day off, reliable as clockwork. Don't go to him for a call out though. Don't involve him in anything like that. Family man is Sammy, pure and simple. Doesn't like to get his hands dirty with any of that stuff does he? Nice fella but definitely not up for it on the larger scale of things. Marvellous.

The waitress comes over and asks me if I would like a refill. Very kind of her and I gladly accept. I need all the caffeine I can get my hands on. Sleep isn't all that forthcoming at the moment and the days can get a little blurry if I don't keep myself fuelled.

This is a very nice place they have here and the staff are actually very friendly. Not in the American style, but just genuinely pleasant in their ways. The one that's been serving me is a delight. She can't be a day over twenty one and she looks like the proverbial English Rose. Lovely smile and slightly rosy cheeks. The kind of girl you'd be proud to call your daughter. I just know that's how molly's going to grow up; the quintessential English Rose, but I can't think about her now. Not right now. Not when I'm going to do what I'm about to do. I have to separate myself from all of that now and centre myself on the job in hand. I need to be focussed when he arrives so I can carry this off from start to finish. I need to get into character completely. It's the only way this will work.

Looking at my watch I see it's ten to one. He's due at one so I call over my charming hostess and order another cup of coffee. Within a few minutes she brings it over with a smile and goes about her business.

I already have the vial in my hand and I break the top off with my thumb and pour the contents into the other cup as if it was the most natural thing in the world. That's the way to do things like this, just be so natural that no one bats an eyelid. I used to know a thief years ago who, when he needed parts to service his car, would go into Halfords or wherever and just take the parts out of their boxes and put them into his pockets so naturally that no one gave him a second thought. He'd always buy something just to provide himself with a bit of cover, but it would only be a set of points or something cheap. Cheeky fucker but it worked for him.

It's worked for me now and the frothy covering has hardly been disturbed. Don't know whether to give it a stir or not. That's a tricky one. That would definitely look tampered with but I don't want the added elixir to sit at the bottom of the cup do I? He might be one of those that doesn't finish his brew and then all this will turn messy and I've had enough of messy.

I pick the cup up and swill the contents around being careful to not let it lap over the sides. That should do it and if it doesn't I'm just going to have to resort to tried and tested methods.

At exactly one o'clock, he bounces through the door in his best trackie and moodiest face.

"Now then Sammy" he greets me as he sits opposite and leans over on his elbows with his best conspiratorial manner "What's this all about then?"

"Alright Finchy lad" I return the greeting "how's tricks?"

"Fine lad, fine. What's goin' on?" he enquires again, eager to find out exactly what's happening and how it involves him "You said something about a deal"

"Yeah mate, something like that yeah. I've got a bit of the other I need to shift and your Terry has recommended your good self as someone who can move things, know what I mean?"

Finchy bridles at this and his ego inflates so much it's pumped up his shoulders. Flattery, works every time.

"You've spoke to him then?" he asks, a look of hope in his eyes.

"A few times yeah"

"When?"

"The other day"

"I can't get hold of the cunt" he informs me "Never has his phone on does he?"

"He's a difficult man to get hold of alright. I got you a coffee there la" I tell him as I point to the cup on his side of the table.

"Nice one" he replies and to my delight, deposits three teaspoons of sugar into the frothy depths and stirs it vigorously. Finchy lad, you fucking legend. You absolute fucking gem.

"So what's the crack with this deal then?" he asks after taking a long swig of his beverage.

"Finish your brew and we'll discuss it in the car. Too many ears around here know what I mean?"

"Yeah la, spot on an' that" he says before chugging down his tainted drink with great gusto.

I get up from the table and go to the counter to pay the bill. The girl that's been serving me comes up with a smile and informs me that I owe £5.60. I give her a twenty and tell her to keep the change and her little face lights up. Bless.

I've no idea how long it'll take for the added ingredient to start to work so it's best that I get Finchy in the car as soon as. It's only parked a little way down the road so I should be able to get him there without any fuss. Marvellous.

"Where are we goin' then?" he enquires as we stroll up the street.

"I've got it stashed in a safe place, we'll go there first and then we can make plans from there. I'm gonna' be trusting you with a large amount here kidder so don't let me down eh?"

"No worries there la, no worries at all, I'm up front me mate, our Terry'll tell you that" he protests but I can see in his eyes that he's looking for an angle here. Looking for a way to screw yours truly if he can. That is a fact. He wants to rip me off if there's a chance.

"Just how much are we talking about here?" he enquires as we get in my car.

"A couple of keys, maybe more. Would that be a problem?"

"Problem? Fuckin' jokin' aren't you? No fuckin' problem here la, no problem at all, I can move that ASAP. No danger. Just you leave it to aul' Finchy. I'll have that moved for you in no time mate, no time at all"

His eyes are positively bulging now. He can almost see the pound signs in front of his beady little eyes and the sight is comical. Fucking hilarious if I'm perfectly honest. This idiot thinks he's in for a nice little dropsy, nice little earner, when, in actual fact, he's in for something completely different. Yes there's a large amount of bugle that needs shifting but you're not going to get your grubby little hands on a single gram of it are you Finchy you stupid fucker? No I've got other plans for you, just as important in the scheme of things, but very different from what you've got in mind.

I steer the car onto Dale Street and down towards the river as the first yawn emanates from his mouth. Oh happy days!

CHAPTER 65

BY THE TIME WE GET to the warehouse, he's completely out of it and slumped against the door. From the outside he must just look like he's having a kip and to a certain extent that's true. The fact that his unconscious state has been brought about with aid of rhohypnol is just between my victim and myself.

I press the button on the fob to open the main door and slowly drive inside as the roller shutter reaches it's zenith.

In seconds I'm out of the car and closing the huge door behind us so as not to attract any unwanted attention. The neon strip lights illuminate the interior with an eerie glow.

I open the passenger door and my fine friend half falls out of the car and I undo his seatbelt to drag him the rest of the way. He's a heavy cunt this fella. Proper dead weight and it's proving difficult to get him to the hatch in the floor, which leads to the underground compartment. His hands are making a squeaking sound as they drag across the polished, painted concrete floor.

I open the hatch and reach around underneath to find the light switch. Where the fuck is it? My hand is searching around frantically but to no avail.

As I'm about to get up and go in search of a torch, a hand clamps on my leg and my heart almost stops in my chest. My head snaps around to see Finchy desperately trying to drag himself to his feet, his eyes going in all different directions, almost cartoon like. A swift kick sends him rolling onto his back, the groans coming from his bleeding mouth almost inhuman. Fucking twat! That put the fear of god into me that did. I'll find the light later, right now I need to get this fucker squared away before he wakes up for proper. With a few heaving steps, I get him to the edge of the opening and roll him inside. The sound he makes as he hits the floor is disturbing to say the least and the thought occurs to me that I might have killed the cunt already. That just wouldn't do. I need the twat alive for the plan to work. A dead Finchy would hold no bargaining power at all and that's no use to anyone.

Panic hits me and I drop to my knees and resume my frantic search for the light switch. Just as desperation threatens to take over, my hand falls upon my intended target and I flick the switch. Quickly looking down I can see Finchy lying at an unnatural angle on the hard floor and he's not moving. Shit. Shit, shit, shit, shit, shit. This is not good. This is not good at all. I quickly lower myself down and drop the final few feet to the floor. Quick as a flash I've got my fingers to his neck, checking for a pulse. It's there, very faint, but it's there. Thank fuck for that! I check his limbs and it looks like his left leg is broken, in fact I'm sure it is. As I move him onto his back, the lower part of his leg stays where it is and the true extent of his injury becomes apparent. This is a Jim Beglin, Djibril Cisse break this one. Snapped in two. This is going to be agony for the poor fucker when he eventually comes round. Lucky I've brought some of the smack with me isn't it? That should numb the pain.

I pick up the rope that I've got stashed down here and proceed to tie him up. Don't want him thrashing around when he wakes up now do I? Could get very out of hand considering recent events and we wouldn't want that.

Once he's trussed up nice and tight I turn to go back up and that's when it hits me. Where's the fucking ladder? My eyes search the surrounding area frantically and my predicament becomes all too clear. There isn't one. I've left it up top, stupid twat! I'm stood here, below the hatch, looking up and it must be nine foot up at least. Panic hits and I leap for the opening but fall short, miserably short. I leap again but to no avail. This is getting worse by the minute. I scan the surroundings again in a manic search for something to stand on, but there's nothing. Not a thing in this deep, dank hole for me to gain any height off. I am Fucked.

Oh Sammy, you stupid twat, what the fuck have you done? What the fuck have you done? You thick, dozy wanker. The ladder la. The fucking ladder! Dead simple isn't it? Dead fucking easy – the ladder. How the fuck else are you gonna' get back up you knobhead? Oh fucking hell, this is very bad.

Slow down lad, think. Just calm it right down and think. There's got to be a way to sort this out hasn't there? Of course there fucking has. There has to be a way, you just have to slow down and think about it, that's all. For god's sake don't panic or you're plain fucked. Pure and simple.

There is definitely nothing to stand on, that is a fact. The place is bear. Completely. You made sure of that yesterday didn't you? There's nothing down here at all save for your good self and this piece of shit tied up in the corner. There is a way though, I know it. I can feel it. There's something staring me in the face and all I have to do is identify it and use it. What is it though? What the fuck is it that I can use to get out of this very shitty situation? There's only me and him isn't there? Just me and him and a whole lot of time, that's all. Nothing else. Completely alone, the pair of us.

I could stand on him to gain a bit of extra height but I can't see that being enough. He's not that fat, unfortunately. He could give me a leg up but why would he, even if he could stand, why would he? There's no way he's gonna' help me do anything when he comes round and realises the real situation. I know I fucking wouldn't if I was in his place and I can't exactly threaten him to do it either can I? He'd probably bite my bollocks off or something when I was half way up.

When he does eventually come round he's going to realise what's in store for him, not even he's that thick that he won't work out what's coming and if that was me, I'd want to take the other fucker with me, know what I mean?

Think Sammy lad, think. There is a way. There is definitely a way, you just have to work it out.

I take my mobile phone from my pocket but I know, even before I've looked at it, that there'll be no signal down here. No chance and I'm proven right as the lack of bars on the left of the screen stares defiantly back at me. Twat.

My legs give way and I slump to the floor as desperation and despair attempt to take over.

Chapter 66

A COUPLE OF HOURS HAVE passed and my captive is beginning the arduous journey back consciousness. He's not fully awake yet, but the look of pain streaking across his face tells of things to come. When he does finally wake up he's going to be in agony and this is the time when I've got to continue with the plan, no matter what else I've got to deal with, I must finish that at least.

I drag myself to my feet and amble over to the far wall where a small sports bag awaits me. I pull out the contents and begin the task of cooking up a hit of heroin. Not too strong, just enough to take away his pain enough for him to perform.

When the shitty brown liquid bubbles, I draw it up into the syringe and hold it vertical whilst flicking the side and pressing the plunger slightly to release any unwanted bubbles. Now I'm ready for him.

The moans are getting louder now and it won't be long before he's completely compos. Don't fancy being in his shoes when he does come round though. The pain is going to be sickening. Good job Doctor Jackson is on hand with a nice painkiller for him isn't it? He'll beg me for this eventually, you just watch.

With one almighty scream he springs back into the land of the living and the drama commences. He's writhing now, convulsing almost as the pain takes over his entire body. Don't think he's even realised I'm here, the agony is so bad. Combined with the fact that he's extremely tightly bound, this must be horrific. He can't even bring his hands round from his back and the terror is clear in his eyes.

He catches sight of yours truly and goes into overdrive.

"For fuck's sake Sammy lad, what are you doin'?" he desperately begs "What the fuck's goin' on?"

"You need to do me a favour Finchy lad and then I'll take away your pain"

"Sammy you twat let me fuckin' go!" he exclaims as his writhing increases to a point where it must be causing him added pain.

"All in good time kidder, all in good time. I need you to do something for me first okay?"

"What the fuck...?" he begins but is interrupted by a stream of vomit that sprouts forth from this swollen mouth.

"Calm yourself down Finchy lad, there's no need for that now is there? You'll just make things worse for yourself that way won't you?"

"Fuck off you cunt" Let me go now you twat, I'm gonna' fuckin' slice you up you fuckin' prick!"

"Nobody's going to slice anybody up now are they? Let's be sensible here. There's no need for any bad feeling is there? Course there isn't. The fact of the matter is my fine friend, that you have a compound fracture of your left leg. A *very* compound fracture if I may make so bold and it's going to require urgent medical treatment. Medical treatment includes pain relief in the form of Diamorphine, do you know what that is?"

He just looks at me through his torment and anguish.

"It's actually pharmaceutical smack lad, is what it is. Pure and simple. Now I'm guessing that the pain is almost unbearable at the moment am I right?"

"AAAAAARRRRGH!" is his curt reply, the scream echoing around the vacant interior of our mutual prison.

"I thought so, so I've brought you a little makeshift analgesic of my own creation" I tell him as I hold the syringe up for his perusal.

"FUCK OFF!" He bellows at me.

"What, you don't want it?" I ask with mock sympathy "Are you sure?"

"FUCKIN' TWAT! Don't bring that anywhere near me!"

"Why Finchy? What are you afraid of? One jab's not gonna' do you any harm is it? And it'll take away all that nasty, sickening pain that's giving you grief won't it?"

"FUCK...OFF!"

"Charming. I offer the hand of assistance and he bites it off. Oh well. We'll just leave it a few hours eh? See how you're getting on then shall we? After all, I'm in no hurry am I? No worries there lad. I've got all the time in the world, so I'll just sit over here for a while and bide my time"

I move over to the other side of the twenty foot square room and sit myself down against the wall. This could be a long night.

"When our Terry finds out about this he'll fuckin' do you" Finchy reliably informs me.

"Will he now?" I reply with little conviction. Time to cut conversation and let him stew in his situation.

"Fuckin' right he will, he'll fuckin' carve you up you cunt. You're a dead man"

"So what does that make you?" I ask and this seems to shut him up. The realisation that he may not be getting out of this in one piece starts to sink in and it's written all over his face. Fear. Pure, unsullied fear. Shouldn't be long now. He'll crack soon then he's mine for the taking.

It only takes half an hour. That's all. He's begging for it now. Really pleading and the sight is pitiful.

"Okay Finchy lad, okay, I'll give you the shot but you're going to have to do something for me yeah? You don't think things like this come for free do you?"

He just looks at me, dumfounded.

"What I want you to do is give a little message for your Terry, that's all. Just a bit of camera work. You can do that can't you?"

"Yesssss" he hisses through his agony "Anything just give me that shit will you"

"That's what I want to hear la. Spot on. Now I'll put you out of your pain, after all, I'm not a monster am I?"

He just looks at me with an expression that tells me if I'm not a monster, I'm something very fucking close.

Chapter 67

I watch the film clip for the third time on the mobile I've recently purchased for this very purpose, and it's perfect. Absolutely spot on if I'm honest. I think I'd give Tarantino a run for his money with this little classic.

Finchy is framed nicely as he goes about his spiel and it's almost word perfect:

"Terry, do what they say lad or they're gonna slice me up, please. Don't let them kill me la, for god's sake, don't let them fuckin' finish me. It's up to you Terry, please help me"

Excellent. The use of the word 'them' instead of him should throw the fucker off the scent. No names are mentioned and no familiar surroundings are present. Marvellous.

He's asking for another hit now and who am I to deny a man mercy? That would be cruel wouldn't it? No, I'm going to give the lad what he wants, only, it's going to be a bit more powerful than the last one. Truth is it'd be enough to put a bull elephant on his arse. I've seen my way out of here and I need to take care of my companion before I can put it into practise. Pity, I had intended on keeping him alive for a bit longer, but needs must.

The veins on his arms are already standing out and the needle sinks beneath the skin with ease. I depress the plunger and watch as his eyes roll back in his head. Goodnight kidder. Sweet dreams.

Chapter 68

I'M PRETTY SURE HE'S DEAD but I'd better check first. Don't want him springing up on me now do I?

As I approach his body the smell of exretia, barely masked by the stench of vomit tells me what I want to know. I check for a pulse all the same.

Nothing. Not a thing. His skin is already beginning to feel colder than it should. Everything has shut down and ceased to work, including his sphincter muscle and the resulting odour is pungent to say the least. He is most definitely a goner, no two ways about that one and I begin the task of untying him.

He must've wriggled some as the knots are extremely tight and take time to undo. All the while, the noxious fumes of his recently opened bowels are playing havoc with my stomach. The urge to vomit myself swells in my gut but I manage to repress it for now and the thought occurs to me that my nausea is being caused by the smell, not what I've done. It would seem that the time when killing someone made me sick has long passed and in all honesty, I can't really say I feel anything about this one, other than relief that I managed to pull it off more or less as planned. The fact that another corpse of my own making lies at my feet doesn't appear to register with me. This is just another step to getting things back in order. That's all. Nothing more. I don't even feel sorry for the fella, can't feel an ounce of sympathy. The way he went about his life, diving into any drug deal presented to him, would have ensured an early grave for the lad and the fact that I am the facilitator of his eventual demise is immaterial. Would've happened sooner or later wouldn't it? Course it would. Accident waiting to happen this fella, no mistake.

As I drag the rope from his prostrate body, it doesn't look as long as I remember and a pang of anxiety runs through my gut. This is the only way out of here and if this doesn't work, it's a long slow death from dehydration, or a hot shot for yours truly.

I've rented this warehouse on a short-term lease for a month. That commenced three days ago so it's going to be quite a while before anyone comes asking questions and what will they find? Fucking rotting, fetid, stinking mess is what they'll find if I can't get this to work.

I tie a loop at one end of the rope and a few knots along it's length for grip. Taking aim at the hole in the ceiling, I lash it up as far as I can and slowly drag it back, hoping that it will find purchase on it's way back to me. It doesn't and the nylon cable falls ungraciously on my head as gravity does it's job.

Again I try, and again it fails to fix to anything substantial.

I try in all different directions turning a complete three sixty and the more it falls back to me, the more the panic heightens in my chest.

This could be it. All that work, all that shit for it to end like this? Surely fucking not.

I continue to cast the rope aloft and it continues to fall back through the opening which is tantalisingly just out of reach.

My heart sinks, my head drops and I slump to the floor. Beaten for now.

CHAPTER 69

As I COME TO, MY predicament escapes me for a second or two as I orientate myself to my surroundings.

Stark reality hits me like a bat and the sinking feeling redoubles it's efforts to empty my innards of their contents.

The reek from the recently deceased Finchy fills my nostrils and wins the final push in the battle as what's left of my stomach contents spring forth in a glorious stream of coffee coloured vomit. I manage to miss my clothes as I heave forwards to facilitate the exodus of everything I've consumed.

When eventually the retching has stopped, I glance at my watch to see it's four in the morning. I've been here nearly twelve hours and my thirst, heightened by my recent heaving, is starting to rage. The beginnings of a dehydration headache are dancing around at the back of my skull and my tongue feels like a piece of leather.

I need to get out of here as soon as or I will lack the strength to climb up the rope even if I get it to stick.

I drag myself to my feet and continue with my fruitless game of lasso. My accuracy is fading and sometimes I can't even get it through the hole and it just hits the ceiling and falls flatly back to the cold concrete floor.

Got to keep on trying though, can't give in. Not now. Not when I've come so far.

CHAPTER 70

DON'T KNOW HOW LONG I tried for last night, but I must've passed out at some stage. It's now ten o'clock in the morning and I'm still here with a dead man for company.

He's gone a horrible colour now, sort of bluish grey if you get my meaning. I don't know if the stench is subsiding or I'm just getting used to it, as it doesn't seem to be attacking my sinuses as much as it was.

I feel drained. Absolutely empty if I'm honest. The urge to just lie down and give up is overwhelming.

Pull yourself together you fanny. What the fuck are you thinking about now? You fucking tart, just get your arse up and carry on trying to snare that rope.

Oh, it's you.

Fuckin' dead right it's me. You don't think I'm just gonna' let you roll over and die do you? Fuck that sunshine, the war is far from over. Get your lazy arse up and get going. Every minute you waste is a minute closer to death you prick, so move yourself.

CHAPTER 71

FIVE PM AND STILL NO joy. My shoulders are aching and my neck's gone stiff from constantly looking up.

My headache has taken hold with a verve and it's piercing my vision. My skin is starting to itch and my mouth is completely devoid of any moisture, but still I continue, repeatedly throwing up the rope and watching it fall back to me.

A couple of times I've been teased by a snag as the rope has caught on something on it's return but nothing substantial enough to take my weight.

Desperation threatens to take over as I'm racked with a fit of sobs. My shoulders positively bounce as my body convulses with grief. I slump to the floor once more and the bag with the smack comes into my line of vision as I come to rest on the cold concrete.

That would be a very easy option now, just load up a mega hit and wave goodbye to the world in a completely painless way. That would take away the piercing migraine and the sandpaper feel to my skin. That would end it all, but that would be too easy.

With a hitherto untapped burst of energy I leap to my feet and cast the rope as hard and as far as I can while still holding on to one end and as I snatch it back it goes taut in my hand. Fuckin' get paid! My heart leaps in my chest and my spirits soar.

Being ever careful not to dislodge it, I put increasing pressure on the rope. The sound that greets me from above is that of something metallic, possibly aluminium, dragging across the floor. I hold my breath as the mystery object approaches the hatch opening and I just hope that it will be large enough to lodge across the hole.

As the end of the rope approaches I catch sight of my saviour for the first time. It's only the fucking ladder isn't it? Fucking bang on! The loop has snagged on one of the storage hooks on the side and has dragged it right across the aperture. I try desperately to jerk it across so that the end of the ladder can fall down to me but all I succeed in doing is freeing the rope and it falls back down with a depressing whump. It's not that bad though. All I need to do now is send the rope around one of the rungs and I can climb out. Dead fucking easy.

After a few attempts I achieve my goal and as the looped end drops over a rung, I jump up to grab it on it's way back down. Quickly placing the other end through the loop I pull it tight and the slipknot effect tightens on the ladder above. I flick the ladder over to one side of the hole so as to give me enough room to get out and begin my ascent.

This is not as easy as I first thought and the strength seems to seep from my tired, aching arms. However, the knots give me something to grab on to and I hoist myself ever so slowly towards salvation.

As my head draws level with the opening, the sigh of relief that escapes me is all too audible and I nearly loose my grip. Quickly steadying myself with my hands on either side of the hatch, I pull myself from hell and flop onto the cold painted floor and wait for my breathing to return to normal.

Fucking get paid.

As my breathing settles, my thirst takes over and I get up and lurch towards the sink in the corner and throw the cold tap open. Sticking my head underneath the glorious stream of crisp, clear water, I take huge, greedy gulps as the beautiful fluid cascades over my face. I don't want to stop. I want this moment to last forever. The feeling of rehydration is amazing and I can almost feel the water seeping through my every cell as it replenishes my depleted body. Heaven. Pure heaven.

CHAPTER 72

BACK IN THE CAR AND on the road back home, I'm made aware of the odour coming from my unwashed body by the confined interior. I need to get back the apartment and scrub all this palaver off my skin and cleanse my tired, aching body.

I turn the radio on and am delighted to hear the headline news. It would appear that legendary hard man and renown local villain Billy Buck has met a sticky end on his very own doorstep. He has been struck in the head by five bullets and was pronounced dead at the scene.

Fucking marvellous. Spot on. Badger, I could kiss you lad, if you weren't so minty.

Apparently police have a few leads and want to question the driver of a blue Ford Focus who was observed loitering around the area prior to the shooting. Even better! Haven't got a clue who the fucker is, but he's just taken the glare well and truly off've Badger.

Things are starting to come together and the loose ends are beginning to be tied up, once and for all. I am definitely on the path back to normality, I can feel it in my bones.

I need to speak to Amy, even if it's just for a minute. Just to hear her voice down the phone would be heaven. Even if she only says hello and puts the phone down. That would be enough for now.

Can't get the kids faces out of my mind. I haven't even seen the face of my newborn daughter and that is killing me as well.

Can't think about that now though, got to concentrate on the job in hand and that is tying everything up so as I can start to try and make amends with my beautiful wife. If she can find it in her heart to forgive me.

CHAPTER 73

I'VE ONLY BEEN STOOD OUTSIDE the Oak for half an hour and I see Badger scuttling up the road with a look of urgency plastered across his grid. This lad's on a mission. He knows that he's in for the pot of gold at the end of the rainbow and he wants it badly. Absolutely driven he is. He can't take his eyes off've my face. He still can't believe that he's going to get his hands on all that luurrrvely tackle.

"Now then Sammy lad" he enthusiastically greets me "I done the biz didn't I?"

"You certainly did Badger, you certainly did. Anybody see you?"

"No chance Sam, in and out wasn't I? Dead fuckin' quick like"

"And you've no idea about this blue Focus they're lookin' for?"

He looks at me with genuine incomprehension. He hasn't got a clue. Good stuff.

"What Focus was that then?"

"Doesn't matter lad"

"You got me parcel then?" he asks me hopping from one foot to another, eager as fuck to see his bounty.

"Oh aye Badger lad. Step into my office" and with that, I lead him down the side street towards my awaiting car.

As I lift he boot lid, the dim interior lights illuminate the brown package like the Holy Grail and Badger's eyes light up like beacons.

"Help yourself kidder" I tell him. I've already wiped my dabs off it with petrol on a rag, so I don't want to touch it again.

Badger snatches it out of the boot like his life depends on it and rapidly secretes it within the multi-layered puzzle that is his clothing.

"Nice one Sammy lad!" he's buzzing now "Any other little jobs you need doin' just ask Badger"

"Will do la. Don't you make a pig of yourself now will you?" I tell him and the grin that splits his face reveals teeth like a row of bombed out houses. Blackened and crooked and broken.

He bids me a fond farewell and scuttles off down the street in the direction he came from.

Sweet dreams Badger lad. That's another job jobbed. Done and dusted. A load off my mind. He won't be causing me any problems in the future. Not with what I've mixed the brown with. In fact, I would guess that he'll be out of the picture within the hour. Happy Days la, happy fuckin' days.

CHAPTER 74

THE PROBLEM I HAVE NOW is getting the unfortunate Finchy out of the underground compartment. I know for certain that I won't be able to lift him on my own. That is a fact. There's no way I'd be able to heave the hefty fucker through that hole on my own. Just wouldn't happen.

There's only one person I could trust to give me a hand but I don't want to involve him anymore than I already have. I know Alfie'd be bang up for it and would back me a hundred and ninety percent, but I don't want to put him deeper into the mire. Accessory to murder would carry a weighty sentence and I just couldn't do it to the lad. I'll have to think of something else and quick. The stench down there must be horrific already.

It's funny, but the Finchy thing is playing on my mind like an unpaid bill. That's all. Like something I've got to do around the house. A room to paint or the lawn to mow. The fact that it's a decaying corpse of my own creation and that I've got to get it out of there before my lease is up, seems strangely bland and slightly annoying. That's all. Nothing more. Just an annoyance, an irritation.

How desensitised have I become? How far from humanity have I drifted? How the fuck did I get to this? Is this how the likes of JJ and Billy Buck have been all their lives? Is this how they were born? With a complete lack of concern for human life? Is this how I was born but just didn't know it? Given different circumstances and surroundings, would I have risen through the ranks to become one of the faces of this city? Would that have been what I would've wanted? What I would've strived for? Is it Nature or Nurture? Am I inherently evil or has my environment thrust me into this way of thinking? It's a question I just can't answer. Or don't want to.

Sitting here in this blandly furnished apartment I'm forced to face my demons again and again. The telly is no distraction and only serves to remind me of my solitude. Any music I play instantly reminds me of Amy, of course it does. Every song I've heard for the last twenty odd years I've been with her. There are so many songs that remind me of different times that I daren't turn on the radio for fear of losing the plot. So I sit here in silence. Alone. Surrounded by the spoils of my actions. The money is all stashed in the utility cupboard. Not very original, but storage space is a bit limited up here in Chez Coca.

The rest of the gear has been secreted in a storage facility not far from here and has no connections to me in any way. Think I might have a buyer for that little lot as well. I know I should just lash it away, but I just can't bring myself to do it. I know if I want to distance myself from all this mayhem I've got to cut all ties and links with the filthy world I've discovered, but if I can just make one more score out of my ill gotten gains, then I might as well. I've got to. It'd be rude not to. Just have to do it, end of story.

I've sent the little film clip with a brief message to Terrance so he should get it next time he turns his phone on. Once he sees that, he'll have no choice but to show his face and then I can truly put all this nonsense to bed.

Through shear desperation and extreme boredom I flick on the box and turn over to the local news. There's a few bits about the Capital of Culture Company, deadlines for 2008 and suchlike, but nothing that grabs my attention.

It's only now that I realise how tired I am. I struggle to keep my eyes open for a while then eventually give in as sleep takes me.

CHAPTER 75

As consciousness greets me the noise from the TV invades my ears and brings me to, somewhat abruptly. It's not the fact that it's any louder than it was but it snaps me back awake all the same.

When I eventually regain full composure I realise that it's the story's content that's grabbing my attention. It would appear that there's a contaminated batch of heroin circulating on the streets of Liverpool and four homeless people have already fell victim to it's toxicity.

Well, well Badger lad. It would seem your generosity has had a devastating effect. I really thought the old tramp would've kept it all for himself to be honest. I didn't even imagine he would be passing on his bounty to his fellow unwashed. Maybe he sold a bit, who knows? All I know is that another part of this bizarre puzzle has been squared away. Done and dusted. End of.

I can now add another four human lives to my running total and I don't feel the slightest bit remorseful about any of them. All's they were is a gang of bagheads. Nothing more. Scum infecting our streets and society. Tainting the face of our beautiful city. An irritation on the very skin of this wonderful, multicultural melting pot. I have done the city a favour.

I look at the clock to see that it's gone ten. I'm late for work but to be honest, I don't think I'll be going in today. Today is a day for me, for cheering myself up. Think I'll go and get a new car today.

The Beamer is going to be known by now by all and sundry in the door industry and anonymity is key if I'm to complete my plans successfully.

Think I'll mosey on down to the Merc garage, see what they have to offer. Quite fancy one of those Jeeps that they do. They look nice in black or silver. Tinted windows'll keep my identity to myself and provide me with excellent cover moving around the city.

I've got the cash in one of the accounts already. I've been trickling it in now for quite a while and nobody has questioned me at all. It'd be a bit on top if I was to walk into a Merc garage and pay for a new four be four with cash now wouldn't it? Might raise a few eyebrows. No, switch will do nicely. I'm sure they'll give me a good price for the Beamer. It's still a decent motor. Low mileage, service history and that. No problems.

Yes, today is going to be a good day

Chapter 76

I'VE JUST HAD A TEXT from Terry and it's made my day even better. He's agreed to a meeting at the designated spot and to be honest, I don't think he's got a Scooby Doo that it's me, I really don't. Fuckin' get paid. Once that's done and dusted, I'm on my way back to a normal life, albeit with a few more quid in my pocket than before.

In a moment of inspiration, I pick up my own mobile, press speed dial 2 and hold the handset to my ear.

After what seems like an eternity she answers.

"Hello?" she says with more than enough trepidation.

"Amy?"

"What do you want?"

"Amy, please don't hang up on me"

"Why?"

"I just need to talk to you for a minute"

"What about Sammy? What is there to talk about?"

Just to hear her speak my name is bliss. To hear the word 'Sammy' come from her beautiful mouth is priceless.

"Amy I've sorted all this nonsense out"

"You've what?" she asks incredulously.

"I've sorted it all out, we're not in danger anymore, it's all okay now"

"What the hell are you talking about? You've brought your victim back to life have you? Is that what you've done? You're not a murderer anymore, is that it?"

"Amy listen…"

"To what Sammy? To what? More lies? More deceit? How can you have sorted anything out? You can't change the fact that you took someone's life can you? You can't take that back no matter what you do"

"Amy I…"

"You what Sammy? There's nothing you can say to change the fact that you're not the person I thought I knew is there?"

"Amy I did it for us" I'm dismayed at how weak I sound.

"You did it for us? You killed someone for us? Can you hear yourself? Your pathetic"

This hurts. Coming from her it stings. To know that the love of my life thinks of me this way is too painful to contemplate. I am scum.

"Amy just let me see you"

"Why? What can you say to my face that you can't say on the phone?"

"I just need to see you. You and the baby"

At this I hear her sob just a little on the other end and the sound alarms me.

"Is the baby okay?" I ask, concern running thick through my voice.

"The baby's fine" she replies as relief courses through my body "She's beautiful"

"Just like her mother" I reply in the hope of lightening the conversation.

"Is that a fact?"

"Amy I'd love to see her, if only for a moment. Please, if you could find it in your heart to just let me see you all I…"

"You'd what? Be eternally grateful? What could possibly make me want to go anywhere near you ever again? Much less bring my children"

Our children Amy, *our* children. My blood rises slightly at this remark. They are my kids as well. All of them and I've got rights.

"Come on Amy don't be like that"

"I'm going to hang up now" she tells me.

"Amy don't, please"

"Don't beg Sammy, it's not your style"

"Amy..." but the line's gone dead.

My heart sinks. My head drops. My soul darkens.

CHAPTER 77

I CAN'T BELIEVE I'VE JUST done that, I really can't.

I am a beast, a bully, an animal. I have sunk to a new low. I have excelled even my own rapidly decreasing threshold of evil.

All he did was ask me for some spare change, that's all. Just walked up and asked me with his filthy, scabby face and his putrid, flaky skin, in clothes that hadn't seen the inside of a washing machine for a dog's age.

And what did I do? Knocked fuck out of him, that's what I did. Don't know for the life of me why, but I absolutely went to town on the poor twat. Right outside Lime St. Station, in broad daylight, on Lord Nelson Street. I just erupted. No reason, no warning, just obliterated the snivelling wretch.

I can still hear his screams now, echoing around my head. Haunting me, signifying what I'm turning into, or what I've become.

I can still smell him on my hands as well. That rank, clammy, heavy odour of the permanently unwashed. It's making me sick. Sick to my stomach. It's permeating me, invading me. Seeping into the pores of my skin. Filling my bones to the very marrow. Becoming a part of me. Becoming the stench of me. The stench of my decay. The stench of my rotting soul.

Back in the flat I dive straight in the shower and scrub at my skin to rid myself of all traces of the atrocity. But still it pervades the air around me, filling my nostrils. Mocking me. Choking me.

Like a crazed Lord MacBeth I scrub on to banish this fragrance from my body, but the more I scrub, the stronger it becomes.

My hands and forearms are glowing red now and I can see traces of blood appearing in places where the skin has worn thin. But still I scrub, and still the reek of decay clogs my airways.

The tears are flowing freely now, mingling seamlessly with the piping hot water from the shower.

I want Amy. I want her here now. I want her to put her arms around me and tell me it's all going to be ok. I want her to hold me and kiss me and make all the bad things go away. I want to see her face as she smiles at me with unconditional love. I want my life back.

I can't remember the last time I saw her smile, the last time *I* made her smile anyway. It all seems so long ago now, so distant, like another time and another life. The pain of loss though, is immediate, and very, very now. It burrows through my body. It strangles me. It stifles me. It envelops me. It fills my entire being to the exclusion of all else.

It's like the first day of school when your Mum drops you off for the very first time and as she walks out the door, you cry and wail like you'll never see her again. Your entire self longs for the safety and sanctity of her warm embrace and the panic rises to throttle you. You struggle and reach for her as she walks up the path, but the calm, overly friendly voice of the teacher tells you that it's all ok and that Mum will be back for you later, but her placid tone only adds to your distress as you watch the car pull out of the car park and out of your life.

Please, please, please, please, please Amy don't let me feel like this. Don't let me rot away here in this sterile apartment. Please ring me. Please let there be a knock at the door and let it be you stood there with a 'let's sort all this nonsense out' look adorning your beautiful face as you glide inside and take me in your arms and make it all ok.

But that's not going to happen. I know it's not going to happen. She has made her position painfully clear. I'm not to see her or the kids.

God, the kids, I daren't even think about kids. If I do I will surely lose it for good. My beautiful children. What would they think about their Dad if they knew the truth? Probably the same as their mother. That I'm not worthy of their time. That I'm a lost cause. That I'm scum. And they'd be right.

CHAPTER 78

I'VE HEARD PEOPLE SAY THAT their lives are unravelling before and until now, I've never quite understood what they meant. Despite my best efforts to keep things together and get back to some form of normality, everything just feels like it's spiralling out of control, as if it's all falling through my hands like sand.

No idea what that was about last night with the tramp and that. No idea whatsoever. One minute I'm walking out of the station with a view to grabbing a swift half on the way back to the flat, the next I'm destroying some poor fucker who's only crime was to ask me for money. No build up, no feelings of aggression or frustration before hand, just straight into horrific violence in a millisecond. I can't believe I am capable of such atrocious behaviour, I really can't. The evidence, however, is overwhelming. I have found a part of me that I never knew existed and it's taking over me in waves, sporadically and unpredictably.

It's weird, one day I can feel lucid and alive, like I'm invincible and all this is completely within my control and sortable, the next I'm being carried down a wild and turbulent river with no hope of reaching the shore before I go over the inevitable waterfall and into oblivion.

My mood swings are so wide, varied and volatile that I never know how I'm going to feel when I open my eyes in the morning. That's how bad it's got. When I wake up, I have to lie there to see what state I'm in before I swing my legs out of bed. Sometimes, when the mood of the day is at it's lowest possible ebb, I don't even bother to get up. Several days have been spent like this over the past few weeks, languishing in bed, trying to block out the world from my tired, addled mind. What a mess? What a weak, worthless mess?

Lying here in bed now, it would be so easy to just roll over and stay here all day. Just blank everything out and leave everything 'til tomorrow. But I know I can't. Today is a very big day in the scheme of things. Today is D-Day if you like. Today will be the culmination of all the filthy, rotten, disgusting events I have been party to in order to get things back on an even keel. Today will be the end to a long and sordid chapter in the life of Sammy Jackson. Thank fuck.

My hand glides under the pillow and closes around the grip of the Glock 17 I have stashed there. It's texture is strangely reassuring and I pull it out and examine it closely. It would be so easy just to put the business end to my temple and pull the trigger. *So* Easy. That'd put an end to all this nonsense and would leave Amy and the kids in a very comfortable position financially.

I turn the barrel towards my face and stare into it's shadowy interior. I know the bullet inside is a hollow point and would do untold damage on impact on any part of the body. I wouldn't feel a thing. It'd literally be lights out. Goodnight Vienna. The urge to take the final step is immense. I can feel my finger around the trigger as the pressure slowly increases. I can see straight down the rifled barrel into the depths of the void. A bead of sweat rolls down my forehead and into my eye, but still I increase the tension on my index finger.

I can feel my heart pounding in my chest, so much so it feels as though it will burst free from my ribcage at any minute. I can hear it pulsing in my ears as the blood races around my body at a phenomenal rate. I'm so nearly there, just another fraction of a millimetre, just the merest, minute amount and my problems are over.

Flashpoint. Breakpoint. The point of no return. Shit or bust.

With a dull thud, the weapon drops from my hand and onto the carpet. The tears well up in my eyes and in an instant I'm a blubbering wreck. Inconsolable. Wailing like a baby. Broken.

CHAPTER 79

AN HOUR HAS PASSED NOW and I'm starting to pull myself together. The tears have subsided and my shoulders are no longer bouncing with the sobs of my despair.

I feel wretched, empty and abandoned. I wish I could put today off, but that's impossible. It's not like phoning into work and saying I've got the flu. It's today or never and never would be far too risky. This is the only window of availability for what's got to happen and if I don't take it I'm finished. I've got to summon the strength from somewhere. I've got to dig deep down inside and come up with the goods.

The mobile on the bedside table chirps at me and as I look at the screen to see who's calling, my heart leaps. Amy's name is staring me in the face. Surely not.

"Hello?" I enquire with enormous trepidation.

"Hello Sam" she replies somewhat resignedly.

"Amy I..."

"Just let me speak Sam okay?"

"Okay Amy, yeah, fine, please talk to me"

"Every instinct in my body is telling me that I shouldn't be doing this Sammy and I can't actually believe that I am"

Thankyou. Thankyou God if there is one.

"I still can't believe what you've done Sammy, I really can't. I can't believe that my Sammy could murder someone in cold blood"

"Amy it wasn't in..."

"Just listen Sammy will you?"

"Okay, okay"

"I just can't believe that you would do something like that without a reason. So I've got to thinking there must be a reason why you've turned into this monster and if it's you it must be a really good one. The Sammy that I know wouldn't get mixed up in this sordid world of drugs and murder, not the Sammy I know. There must be a reason and I want to know why Sammy, before we throw all this away for good, I want to know why"

"Amy, I'll tell you everything"

"Not on the phone Sammy, I can't do this on the phone"

My heart positively soars at this piece of news. She wants to see me. She wants to fucking see me. Halle-fucking-luyah she wants to see me.

"Where then?" I ask. The eagerness in my voice barely masked.

"I'll come and see you at the house tonight"

Shit. Not good, not good.

"What time?"

"Eight o'clock"

Bollocks. That's going to be tight. What with the other thing, it's going to be *really* tight. I don't want to risk her going back on her suggestion by asking her to make it a bit later so I'm just going to have to make sure I'm bang on time with the other thing.

"Eight o'clock's fine" I tell her in my calmest tone "I can't wait to see you"

"Don't Sammy. This isn't over yet, not by a long chalk. If you think we're just going to fall into each other's arms tonight you're very much mistaken do you understand?"

"Yes, but..."

"No buts Sammy. There's a very long way to go until things could be anything like they used to be"

"But it's not impossible is it?" I ask of her.

There's a pause on the other end. After what seems like an eternity I hear the response I've been praying for.

"No Sammy, it's not impossible"

I want to bounce off the walls, I want to scream out her name, I want to burst through the ceiling. This is the ray of light that's going to see me through. This is what's going to carry me through today's little saga and out the other side. I'm elated, I'm delighted, I'm euphoric. Victory is mine. I have returned from the land of the dead. I am risen. I am alive. Long live the fucking King.

"Amy I love you so much"

"Don't Sammy, not yet. I can't think like that now. I need to get over this before I can start to think of us as anything more. Do you understand?"

"Of course I do babe, of course I do"

The more she speaks, the more she's giving me indications that there's a way back and the more my spirits rise. It's all going to be okay. I can feel it now. I can almost taste it. It's all going to be okay and I can't contain my sense of relief. The tears are starting to roll down my face now but for a vastly different reason than before. I'm going *home*. Back to what I know and love, back to where I belong.

CHAPTER 80

I'M IN THE NEW MERC and I'm buzzing. From head to toe I'm positively pulsating with the shear joy of it all. I'm on my way back. This is a definite. I'm on my way back. Back to a life more ordinary. Back to what I've cultivated and nurtured for most of my life. Back to the warm and loving heart of my beautiful family.

I want to open the tinted windows and scream in elation as I sail along Dale Street and take a left into Sir Thomas Street.

The traffic lights at Victoria Street bring me to a temporary halt and I gaze across at Ned Kelly's. I want to tell anyone who'll listen how I feel. I want to climb the Radio City Tower and tell the world I'm alive.

Green light and I'm off up towards the Birkenhead Tunnel roundabout. There's a few hackneys about and they're clogging up the outside lane but I don't care. I just wait until they're out of the way and glide over to take the lane up towards Scotty Road. Nothing can annoy me today. Nothing. I am bullet proof today. Fucking immortal. My temper has left the building for the foreseeable future and the sense of euphoria left in it's wake is overwhelming.

I know I can sort this out in time to get back to the house and meet Amy, I'm certain of it. All it'll take is a strict conviction to stick to the plan. That's all. Dead fucking easy. I know I can do it. After all, there's only one thing to do today, that's all. I can clear up another day. That's not a problem. Just need to make sure everything goes like clockwork and I'm home and hosed. Done and dusted. Easy peasy lemon squeezy.

I'm on fire now. The blood is raging around my veins and arteries like Schumacher on speed. I am invincible. Untouchable. Unfucking-believable. I can see the light at the end of the tunnel and for once, it's not a freight train coming the other way.

Can't wait to see her stunning face. That smile and the warmth that flows from her eyes. She truly is a vision. A latter-day saint if ever there was one. She is amazing and it's only now that I truly appreciate how blessed I have been to have had such a person in my life. It's a cliché I know but it's true; you really don't know what you've got until it's gone and to get a second bite of the cherry, well, it's a godsend isn't it?

I know it'll take a while to get back to where we were, but I know it's possible and I'm nothing if not patient.

I can't wait to see the kids and my new baby daughter. The thought of this brings a lump to my throat and I have to choke back the tears as the gorgeous faces of Molly and Connor float into my mind. I wonder what they've been thinking about their Dad not being around. I know Amy will have told them something that will satisfy their curiosity and not have put me in a bad light, after all, it'd only hurt them to know that their Dad was a nasty man wouldn't it? No, she would've been very diplomatic when it came to dealing with the kids I know she would.

Heading up Scotty Road now and I'm slowing down for the speed camera just after the Wallasey Tunnel. I need to bring myself back to the task in hand before I get too carried away. There's still some nastiness to be done before I can truly relax and slip back into my little world of domestic bliss and I can't afford to let anything cloud my judgement, not when I've come so far.

Sat up here in the Merc four-be-four, I feel elevated from the surrounding roads and buildings. The run down outskirts of this ancient city are a million miles away from me as I head up towards the Halfy and the 'peaceful' suburbs thereafter.

County Road is surprisingly empty and most of the traffic lights are on green as I cruise through at as reasonable a speed as I can manage, considering my eagerness to get the day's business over and done with.

As I pass by I gaze at the people on the pavement going about their everyday lives, doing their shopping, trudging from one place to another. I wonder if any of them have sailed as close to the wind as I have these past few months? Are any of them in any way as aware of the sinister side of human life?

Some of the gaunt, gangly characters dressed in trackies, bouncing down the road, look as though they might like to know what it's like. Wannabes they are. Aspiring to be what I despise. Wanting to be known as a name. Desperate to rise above the shit pile that is their everyday. I'm possibly being a little judgemental here but I know it's true. I've seen these characters strutting around town when I've been on the doors. I know their mentality. I can see their desires. I can see their inevitable end. Front page of the Echo. Lad shot dead. Terrible shame for the family. He never done nothin' to nobody. Not fucking much.

I'm on Rice lane now and the prison passes by on my left. I bet there's a fair few of the hoodie brigade in there wondering where the fuck they went wrong and how did they end up in there being brutalised by some big evil grock. Fuck 'em. Not my problem. Deserve all they get.

After today I'm retiring from this sordid little world, that is for certain. There'll be a few bits and pieces to clear up afterwards but they're just incidental. The main business of the day will be my parting shot if you like, pardon the pun, then it's back to utopia for Mr Sammy Jackson, thank you very much. Over and out.

The venue for today's little event has already been arranged, but I need to get there a bit early to make sure everything is in order. Can't leave anything to chance now can I? Got to play the congenial host. It's only right.

The phone chirps up from it's holder on the dashboard and I press the button to answer.

"Alfie lad, how the fuck are you?" I enquire using the hands free.

"Sound la"

"Everything set?"

"Oh aye, done and dusted. No dramas"

"You're a fucking legend Alfie lad, a bonifide legend"

"You gonna' be here on time?" he enquires.

"On my way now, just by the Black Bull"

"Nice one, it's all set out like you said"

"No problems with the van?"

"It's where you wanted, keys are on the front wheel"

"And the lock on the back door's been cracked?"

"Yeah" he replies "all you have to do is push it and the van'll be right outside"

"Spot on kidder, I owe you for this"

"Fuckin' hell la, you more than paid me for the last job"

"And I'm going to pay you for this one as well. You still alright to take the other thing up to Newcastle?"

"Yeah mate, no probs. I'll be on my way as soon as you get here"

"Nice one. I've got you one of those sat-navs so you don't get lost"

"Happy days. See you in a bit" and the phone goes dead.

What a fella? What an absolute, million percent, top notch fella? Asks no questions, tells no tales. Fucking bang on. He's the only person I could trust with a job like this, the only person on this planet if I'm perfectly honest. I've told the connection in Newcastle to expect him this evening and all being well, we should've moved all the remaining gear by tonight to the tune of nigh on half a mil. Fucking get paid. Very nice little earner even if I do say so myself. I can honestly say that, in business, I've had worse days. I really have. This will be the final act of Sammy Jackson – Drugs Baron. This will put a very lucrative full stop to my illicit activities once and for all. Then it's back to civvy street for yours truly. Albeit with a bit more poke in my back bin than I had before, but that's not a bad thing is it? Just one last thing to do first. One last act of iniquity. One last atrocity. Shouldn't be too hard. I've been building myself up to it now for quite a while and I'm ninety nine percent sure I'm ready for it.

Chapter 81

As I turn the corner on the rough, unadopted road, the barn looms up large in my windscreen. It's always been a foreboding place for me ever since I was a nipper. Unused for years, it has a desolate, untouched feel about it that suggests you could die here and nobody would ever know.

As I draw nearer, Alfie's car comes into view. I knew he wouldn't let me down. Fucking Legend. No back answers.

In an instant I'm out of the car and into the murky interior of the ancient building. Sitting in front of me, casually smoking a Number One, is Alfie.

"Now then!" is his cheerful greeting.

"Alfie, what can I say?"

"Think nothing of it me old mucker. The tackle in your boot?"

"Yeah mate, all parcelled up and ready to go"

"Fuckin' bang on. No time like the present eh?" he tells me as he springs to his feet and slaps me on the shoulder.

Back outside, the cargo is moved from car to car with the minimum of fuss.

"That's some amount you've got there kidder" he says as the last bag goes into the boot of his Peugeot estate.

"I know la, it'll be some amount of dough you'll be picking up for it as well. You sure you're alright with all this?"

"No problems la. Consider it done"

"Happy days" I reply with a smile. I don't know why I didn't bring the lad into the business side of all this a lot sooner. He's cool as the proverbial cucumber. Nothing fazes him at all. Spot on.

"There's a few of the lads off've the ship livin' up them ways so I'll nip in to see them while I'm up there" he informs me and at this I can't deny I have a pang of concern.

"You sure that's wise?" I enquire.

"It'll be fine la, don't worry. It'll be after the drop so the gear'll be well gone by then"

"Yeah but if your car gets nicked there's gonna be some Geordie joyriders who're gonna have a very pleasant surprise if you get my meaning"

"No worries la, the lad I'm going to see has got security gates and everything. Made a mint on the property didn't he. Big time Charlie the fucker is nowadays so we're safe as houses"

"Alright la, it's up to you"

"No danger mate. Done and dusted"

"I'll weigh you in when you get back, but here's a few quid to keep you going 'til then" I tell him as I hand him a wad of notes.

"And what the fuck am I going to do with all this, hire a chauffer?"

"Just take it and shut the fuck up," I tell him with a smile.

Things are so nearly over with I can almost taste the flavour of freedom on my tongue. As Alfie drives away down the dirt road I'm overcome with a feeling that everything's going to be okay. It's all going to go to plan and after today I'm out of this horrible, sordid little world and back to reality. Back to being an ordinary Joe with fuck all to prove and no-one to watch out for. Heaven. Pure Heaven. Don't know for the life of me how fellas live their whole lives like this, I really don't. These past few months of constantly looking over my shoulder have taken their toll and I feel I've aged ten years at least.

Time to put the penultimate piece of the jigsaw in place. Time to lay the bait and set the final trap.

I fish the new, pay-as-you-go mobile out of my pocket, type in my present location and send it off for the perusal of Mr Terrance Quinn Esq.

I've previously told him to be waiting in Town today so he'll be half an hour away at least. Plenty of time to get into position and await my prey.

I've already picked my spot. Deep in the undergrowth at the side of the dirt road so as he'll have to come past me to enter the barn. Once his back's to me I've got him. No danger. I'll just follow him in and even if he hears me coming, he won't have time to turn around, no chance. Candy from a baby.

CHAPTER 82

I TELL YOU WHAT, IT's fucking freezing down here in the bushes. Now as I've been still for a while the cold has seeped into my bones and I'm shivering like a baghead.

I've got all angles covered here. There's absolutely no way anybody can arrive unexpectedly. There's only two ways into this place and the other is dead ahead and I can see all the way down the track to the main road. I'm in the best possible position to view all or any movement in any direction.

The gun feels like a block of ice in my hand and I have to pull my sleeve down over my knuckles and the handle to sustain any sense of feeling in my frozen fingers.

Shouldn't be long now. If he was where he was supposed to be, he should be arriving anytime now. A pang shoots through my guts and the thought that this is very nearly the end to all the shit sends a wave of heat through my icy veins. Once this is done, I can shoot down the road to meet Amy at the house. I'm less than a mile away so it shouldn't prove a problem. Just have to make sure that I stand a good distance away from my target so as I don't get any blood spatter on my clobber. Shouldn't be too difficult. I've only ever fired one of these things from close quarters but a few more feet shouldn't make a difference should it?. How difficult can it be?

I wish he'd fucking hurry up though. I want to get this all done and dusted as soon as. Don't like to be hanging around. Haven't got the patience.

A flash of colour catches my eye and I scan through the foliage to try to identify it's origin. It takes a couple of seconds to register but it's him, I'm sure of it. Strolling down the track with his hoodie pulled up over his head, shoulders hunched, walking on his toes. That's him. No two ways about it. Fucking spot on. Come on Terry lad, just keep on walking, that's it, keep going, nice and easy.

He's level with me now and I can see his breath bellowing out of his mouth in great plumes of white as he marches on by. Never seen me though. No chance. I'm fucking invisible.

He's nearly at the barn door now and I'm out of the bushes and following him soundlessly. I'm on fire. I am a fucking ninja. I'm silent and very fucking deadly.

He turns into the gaping, dark doorway and I'm on my toes and off into a sprint, reaching the door myself in milliseconds. The transition from light to dark takes it's toll at first but my eyes quickly adjust. He's there, right in front of me, still walking deeper into the depths of the dilapidated building.

"Put your hands above your head petal" I tell him as I raise the shooter in his direction.

Silently, his hands go up and he just stands there.

"Turn around very slowly" I tell him but he doesn't move.

"D'you hear me kidder, I said turn around"

Still nothing.

"Terry turn the fuck around now!" I yell as frustration combined with an overload of adrenalin nearly gets the better of me.

Slowly, but surely, he turns around but as his face comes into view I'm hit with a daunting realisation. This is not Terry. Shit! I recognise the face but I can't think from where.

Panic hits as the situation slides out of my control. Who the fuck is this? Whoever it is his face is filled with malice and it's most definitely directed towards yours truly.

"What the fuck's going on?" I enquire as I level the gun at the mystery guest's head.

"Funny you should ask kidder" comes a familiar voice from behind me, "put the gun down before somebody gets hurt"

Terry, you sneaky twat. You sneaky, shady little twat.

"Now then Terry lad" I greet him with as calm a tone as I can muster "Long time no see"

"Isn't it just, put the gun down"

Slowly I place the pistol on the floor and turn around to face my adversary. He's smiling. He's smiling the smile of the victorious.

I could try to bluff my way out of this but it would be pointless. Terry's no mug. He knows the score and he well and truly knows it's me that's set this little tete a tete up. It would be an insult to the lad to try and protest my innocence now.

"I gather our Finchy won't be joining us?" he asks of me.

"No" is all I can answer.

"I thought not. Not your way that is it? You like 'em dead don't you? Less hassle that way"

I can't reply. I can't possibly reply.

"But that's none of my concern that now is it?"

"Eh?" I reply somewhat confused at his apparent lack of distress at the news of his cousin's demise.

"You don't really think I'd come all this way back and risk life and limb for that no-mark do you? Give me some credit at least"

The world is tilting sideways and I'm in danger of falling off the edge. This wasn't how this was supposed to go at all. This has all gone to ratshit.

The sound of a car approaching broadens the smile on Terry's face.

"Ah" he grins "the cavalry" and to my horror Alfie's car enters the barn with Eddie Maddox, the doorman off the Bar Bella, at the wheel. This is not good. This is most definitely not good. Where the fuck is Alfie?

I don't have to wait too long for my question to be answered as Eddie bounces out of the car and gleefully opens the rear door. Alfie's bruised and battered body half slumps out as his broken forearms and the side of his head come to rest on the dusty floor.

You cunt Terry, you fuckin' cunt, you didn't have to do this. You didn't have to have the poor twat brutalised. You're gonna' pay for this one my old friend, you mark my words.

The thoughts raging around my stricken mind threaten to burst free, but I manage to keep my composure.

"Now then Sammy lad!" Eddie cheerfully greets me "How the fuck are you?"

"Can't smile wide enough" I reply with as even a tone as I can manage.

"Lovely day for it isn't it?"

"Oh aye" I agree "fantastic"

"It's all there in the boot" he tells Terry with unmasked enthusiasm "Just like you said"

"Marvellous" he beams "You remember Michael Carter don't you Sam?"

My mind is spinning now as I turn my attention to the other fella in the hood, the one I followed into this snare in the first place. The penny drops. It's the lad from the night on the Bar Bella. The brother of the poor unfortunate girl I left in the Jamie Buck's house to burn.

As I turn full circle I'm met with the hardest right hook I've ever felt and my knees buckle. A second quickly follows and I'm on the floor with no idea which way is up. I'm stunned. Temporarily blinded, but this doesn't stop the torrent of violence as kick after kick lands on my unresisting body. I'm done for. Defenceless. I'm at his mercy and judging by the ferocity of his attack I don't think there will be any.

From somewhere miles away I hear Terry's voice calling my assailant to order. To my huge relief, the beating ceases and I'm left to my own devices for a few blissful seconds. Consciousness threatens to leave me to it and I have to struggle to keep myself in the here and now.

As my vision returns, my gaze is met by the cold empty eyes of Alfie's corpse staring straight at me. The unnatural angle of his neck so disturbing as to make my stomach retch. I hold on though. The urge to spew my guts is overwhelming but I hold on. The blood is flowing freely from my nose and broken lips and onto the dirty floor, the bright crimson darkened by the murky colour of the dust as it mingles together. I can feel my eyes swelling from the torrent of physical abuse I have just received.

Terry comes into view above me.

"Now then flower, you've made a right mess here haven't you? Tut, tut. Naughty boy"

I can see his smile spread wide across his face. It's the smile of the cat that knows he's got the mouse exactly where he wants it and it's all just playtime from here on in.

The thought of attack flits through my mind but I haven't got enough left in me. I'm powerless. Just like Anthony Jacobs, just like Jamie Buck. My life is in his hands.

"You still with us Sammy?" I hear Terry enquiring from somewhere a long way off as I drift ever so slightly in and out of consciousness. A groan is all I can muster in reply.

"So what was the plan then kidder eh? Plug me, have me disposed of somewhere convenient and live happily ever after? Sorry Sammy lad, close but no cigar. Just is not gonna' happen I'm afraid. No possible way.

The dough from the little haul in your poor deceased friend's motor would've amounted to quite a tidy sum I'm sure. Large enough to see you into your autumn years eh?"

I can't reply. My jaw refuses to work. I'm completely immobilised. But still he continues.

"What d'you think to my little crew then?" he continues "It's always good to keep in touch isn't it? Got to keep your finger on the pulse haven't you? There's no way I would've trusted that gobshite cousin of mine to keep his ear to the ground and his mouth shut. Just would not've happened. Liked being the gangster too much did our Finchy, wanted to be a name. Wanted to be seen as being the boy. Fucking prick's paid for it now and don't worry Sam, I don't hold it against you. If it wasn't you it would've been someone else. Pure asking for it the lad was, no two ways about it. Only a matter of time and all that. You've done me a favour really, the cunt was a weight around my neck if I'm perfectly honest. Prize whopper. Did you know that the bizzies have found him? It was on the radio before. Well, I presume it's him. A badly mutilated body found in an underground compartment in a warehouse not far from here. Sounds about right doesn't it? Sounds like your M.O. Police are looking to interview the man whose name is on the lease. That'd be you wouldn't it Sam?"

This piece of news tears through my like a rapier. I'm bang to rights on this one, no back answers. There's no explaining my way out of this. Even if I do get out of here alive, I'm well and truly fucked, but the look in Terry's eyes tells me that dead bodies in warehouses are the least of my worries right now.

"There's only one course of action open to me now though isn't there Sammy lad? Like you used to say, got to tie up all loose ends and in all fairness, you're one fuckin' huge loose end aren't you fella? One big, mad liability on more than one count. If you don't try and slot me, you'll be likely to inform the plod of all our little business transactions to get yourself a lighter sentence and that just can't happen. No, there's only one thing I can do la, I'm sure you'll understand. No hard feelings and that but you know how it is, business and all that"

I have no bargaining power, nothing to barter with. I am fucked. This really is the end of the road here for yours truly and the realisation is horrific. To know you're going to die, to leave this world in the next few minutes is unthinkable.

Rodney's face swims up in my mind and his expression the second before I hit him with the wheel brace. The sheer terror of the inevitable. I can feel it now. It's gripping me completely.

I'm staring at the pistol in his hand as he raises it towards me. Just as the skin on his finger starts to change colour with the applied pressure, his mobile phone rings in his pocket.

"Fuck's sake" he curses as he fishes it out and looks at the screen.

"Hello H" he beams as he puts it to his ear "How the fuck are you?"

His smile broadens as he lowers the gun.

"Don't you worry sunshine" he replies after a pause, "it's all in hand. The goods should be with you within the hour" and he gestures to Eddie to get into Alfie's car.

"Yeah, yeah, A friendly face'll be along with it shortly. Yeah, no probs la yeah. I'll see you in the usual for tea and Tiffin later. Nice one"

As he puts the phone back in his pocket he returns his gaze to me.

"That was Mr Haynes in case you didn't know. We've got a bit of an arrangement going which is gonna' be quite lucrative. Nice of you to clear the decks so to speak. With all of the other gobshites out of the way, the city's wide open and it'd be rude not to step in wouldn't it?"

His expression is bordering on maniacal now as he laps up the enormity of the situation. He is positively buzzing in his victory.

"Eddie, take the motor to the big fella, I'll follow you in a bit" he tells his accomplice.

"Right you are kidder" Eddie replies through the open window of my poor dead friend's jalopy and reverses out of the barn and out of the immediate situation.

"Now" he continues as he raises the pistol once more, "where were we?"

I can see down the gapping hole of the barrel and I know my seconds are numbered.

"It's a shame it has to be like this Sammy lad, it really is. You're quite the player when you get going aren't you? Ruthless little cunt if I'm honest. Stone cold killer. I could've done with you on the firm for what's coming next. Still, never mind eh?"

His finger is closing around the trigger again and I can see the pressure building up. My eyes shut instinctively and my whole body tenses in preparation for the bullet which will rip through my body, shredding vital organs as it goes. I hope I die quick. Please God say it'll be over quick.

My body convulses at the sound of the bang and my legs fail me as I hit the deck, desperately searching my torso for the entry hole. I can't find it though. I can't find it despite my best efforts and there's no blood that I can feel or see anywhere. What the fuck is going on?

Terry's laughing jolts me from my fit of panic.

"Steady on there la" he chortles "Anyone'd think you'd been shot"

It's only now that I see the prostrate body to my left. Michael Carter is lying motionless in an ever expanding pool of his own dark red blood. My mind starts to do somersaults. What the fuck is his plan here?

"What's up Sam, cat got your tongue?" he enquires as I drag myself to my feet.

"What the fu...?" I start to ask but I'm brought short by the sight of the smoking barrel levelled at my chest once more.

"What's up?" he asks again and I turn and gesture towards the now deceased Mr Carter, the power of speech having abandoned me for the time being.

"Oh him? Fuckin' moody twat la wasn't he? Wasn't what you'd call company material, not a team player, know what I mean? There wasn't really any room for him in the new firm and he's seen too much already. Never really liked the lad if I'm perfectly honest, bit of a beaut' to be fair"

"And you say *I'm* a stone cold killer" I reply as I find my voice once more.

"Loose ends la, can't have 'em can we? You taught me that if nothing else"

The thought of begging for my life crosses my stricken mind, of pleading that we could still form a formidable alliance and run the city together, hand in glove, but then the situation with Finchy's body and the police spears through my thoughts. What would be the point? Even if I were to get out of this alive I'm looking at a hefty stretch for murder. The chance with Amy would dissipate like smoke in a hurricane. My life would be over anyway.

"Go on then" I tell my leering captor "Get it over with"

"All in good time" he smirks "All in good time"

My temper starts to rise within me, shoulder barging my fear out of the way in no uncertain terms.

"Pull the fuckin' trigger if you're going to" I tell him, the anger flushing my face.

"Steady on there Sammy lad, remember who's in charge here"

"Bollocks, you couldn't run a bath you spineless fuckwit, never mind run a city. You'll get plugged before the month's out you useless pile of shite"

This has the desired effect and his composure starts to slip.

"Shut the fuck up Sammy!" he barks but I've got him now.

"Or what? What the fuck are you going to do you fuckin' faggot? You're a waste of space and I wouldn't trust you to take the dog for a walk never mind look after a large scale deal like the one you've just entrusted to Eddie Maddox. Eddie Maddox la? Of all people? You've just sent that beak head off with half a mil's worth of tackle. You need your head testin' you mate"

"What d'you mean?" he stutters, panic showing as he loses the high ground.

"Do you know how many keys are in that boot?"

"Well no, but…"

"But fuck all. He'll well have his grubby little mitts all over it won't he? He'll either tax it for a couple of bags or just fuck off with the whole lot and you've just given him the ideal opportunity to do whatever he wants"

His mind is ticking over now, going through the possible scenarios that could be happening to his precious merchandise as we stand here chewing the fat.

"He'll be fine la, he knows who he's dealing with"

"What? You and H? Fuckin' hell la you're hardly Ronnie and Reggie are you?"

Concern flashes across his face in waves and I know I've got him. Fuck him. I'm not going to go out like some snivelling wretch pleading for my pathetic life, bollocks to that. If he's gonna' kill me he's gonna' kill me. I'm fucked all ends up now whichever way things turn out. I'm done for. Finished. Finito. The game is over and I don't have enough points to make it to the next level. Pure and simple. I can feel my shoulders pull back and my body straighten as my newfound confidence surges through my now crystal clear mind. Fuck him. Fuck them all. If this is the last chapter in my life then let's have it.

"Sammy, I think you're forgetting who's got the upper hand here kidder" he says with a smile, his poker face resumed momentarily.

"And how's that? You're gonna' plug me whatever I do and to be honest, it's the only way things can go for me now so fuck you. Shoot me you prick, come on…COME ON!" I scream at him and he flinches at the sound.

"Come on you maggot fuckin' shoot me!"

He goes to reply but he can't get a word in.

"Come on Terry lad, fuckin' do it. Terry Quinn eh? What a joke? Who the fuck are you? You're not a name are you? You're not a face in this city. Just another little rat with a pocket full of tackle and no clout with anybody. You're not big enough to run this city la, not by a long way. You're nothing and you'll die on the street like the

252

rest of them, shot by some little seven stone knobhead in a hoodie and bad trainers. That's your future la and you're welcome to it"

He's shaking now, such is his anger at the words coming from me, his intended victim. The person who should be begging for his life.

The pistol is pointed straight at me and I'm waiting for the ring of the shot. Waiting for that piercing bullet to penetrate my unresisting body.

I move towards him and he backs off a little, but I quicken my step and reach out to grab the barrel, fully expecting to hear the deafening bang but surprisingly it doesn't come. I look deep into my would be assassin's eyes and all I can see is terror mixed with confusion. This isn't the way things should be going as far as Terrance is concerned and it's thrown him. All he has to do is pull the trigger and it's all over. Just squeeze that little piece of metal and the situation is resolved, but he doesn't.

"Pull the trigger" I tell him in as calm a voice as I can muster as I hold the gun to my stomach, but he just stands there gripping the shooter that's the only barrier between us.

"Kill me Terry lad, go on, kill me" Still nothing. He is dumbstruck.

"PULL THE FUCKIN' TRIGGER!" I scream and almost instantly I'm rewarded with the glorious, rapturous, voluminous report of the gunshot. My body reacts as if I've been kicked in the stomach by a race horse and I'm thrown to the ground like a rag doll. My vision is filled with Terry's horrified face as he takes in the sight before him. I know what's troubling him though, what's giving him the horrors. It's the fact that I'm smiling. No, more than that, I'm positively beaming.

He's backing away now, back towards the door of the barn. Back towards some kind of sanity. My eyes follow him and just as he's about to leave this, my mausoleum, I mouth the words "Thank you" and then he's gone.

The pain arrives rapidly in my gut, accompanied by a heat so intense, it feels as though I'm on fire. I'm rolling over now. Over and over but there's no escaping the agony. It's planted squarely inside me, burning me from the inside out. It's unbearable, unbelievable. I'm praying for death to take me now, to save me from this agony. I want to feel the cold hand of the reaper on my shoulder as he guides me to whatever's waiting in the next life if there is one. But there's no release, not yet. Right here and now I'm forced to endure this torment as my own life's blood spills over my hands and onto the dusty floor. I can't believe how much there is. It's everywhere. All around me. Surely it can't all be mine, but it must be. It's all over my arms and it smears down my cheeks as I clamp my hands to my face in an effort to block out the horror of it all. But there's no escape. Not this time. Not for a long time. I'm in for the long haul here and I can't escape.

This must be hell. Purgatory at the very least. The fire raging inside me feels like the furnace of Hades and there's no way to quell it. All I can do is ride the storm and keep rolling, over and over.

I'm brought to a halt sharply as I roll into something and I turn to see my friend's battered and bruised corpse, staring at me blankly. Alfie lad I'm so sorry. I never meant it to turn out like this.

Back I roll, over and over, the pain indescribable as it spreads through my entire body. Please God take me now. I can't stand this anymore, please take this away, take me away. Get me out of this pleeeease!

My sight is dimming now, tunnel vision. Everything's closing in. Just a smoky grey tube to peer through. Although there's no sound I know my hearing is diminishing as well. This must be it. Please say this is it. I want to go now. Don't want to hang around anymore. I'm done here, job and knock. I've got my cards and I'm on my way. See you later Sammy lad, mind how you go.

Fire's dying down now, burning itself out. Pain's on it's way too. Warmth replaces heat. Real warmth though. Cosy, beautiful warmth. Elation washes over me and I'm euphoric. This is it. This is the end of it all. The full stop to the maddest chapter in my insignificant, little life. My swan song. I'm on my way...

EPILOGUE

CONSCIOUSNESS RETURNS AND THE SIGHT that greets me is a gruesome one.

How did it come to this? How did I allow myself to get to this point? These are questions I just can't answer.

To make any sense of it all I need to go back to a time when things were ordinary, to a time when I was ordinary, but everything's changed so much now that it's hard to remember the way I was before all this started.

They say ignorance is bliss, out of sight out of mind, what the eye doesn't see, the heart doesn't grieve over, but I've done more than my fair share of grieving if the truth be known. I grieve every day, for the people I've lost and the life I've squandered. I grieve for the part of me that was naïve to this side of life which I now find myself consumed by.

I don't suppose I'm making much sense here and you'd be forgiven for thinking I'm a little unhinged. Truth is you may be right. Truth is I've seen and done things from which there is no return.

Was I ever ordinary or was this part of me lurking beneath the surface, waiting to emerge at the appropriate time? Would I have lived my life never knowing of my other side if I had not made the choices I did?

And how simple those choices were. No long contemplation, no great deliberation. I made my choices simply and quickly with no apparent regard for the consequences and no conception of the fallout that would inevitably ensue. But that's me all over, act first, ask questions later. Impulsive isn't in it.

The blood's starting to dry now. It's russet hue covering my hands and forearms. I can feel it hardening on my face as it oxidises and clots.

There's no way back from this. There's no way I can ever live a normal life again, not knowing what I know now. Not having done what I've done and seen what I've seen. But I can't complain. It was all of my own doing, all my own choice and now I must take the consequences.

I didn't expect to wake up again. I thought I would be on my way, but here I am, still in the land of the living. I'm so cold though, despite the thick winter coat that surrounds me, I'm shivering. My bones feel like ice and movement is so very difficult. There must be more of my blood on the grimy, dusty floor now than there is left in my body. I'm beyond repair. Surely it won't be long now.

Looking at my watch I'm met with the bluish grey colour of the skin on my arm. The colour of a corpse.

It's very nearly eight o'clock. Amy will be at the house now, I know she will. She's always early. My beautiful wife. My best mate. I've let you down so badly. Can't bear the thought of you waiting there in that empty house, full of anticipation and hope. The disappointment you have to come will be crippling and you really don't deserve a bit of it. It's all my fault though. One hundred percent down to me and my shitty bad judgement. Please find it in your heart to forgive me my love. I did it all for you Amy, I did it all for you...

Lightning Source UK Ltd.
Milton Keynes UK
171292UK00001B/20/P